U0141908

我的第一本
親子英文字典

CHILDREN'S DICTIONARY

多功能字典
查詢、背誦一本搞定

近來，小學學生普遍都能說上一、兩句英文，幼稚園和小學課程也都已經開始實施英文教育。

不過，在台灣大部分的學習環境，學習英文並不像學習中文那樣，能夠靠耳濡目染，自然而然地體會，所以在單字的認知方面比較缺乏正確性。

而且，當我們翻開英文字典，發現龐大的單字量，就會退避三舍。所以，對於英文學習較容易產生反感是不爭的事實。

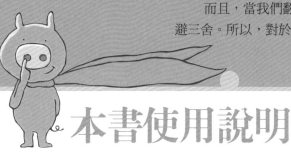

本書使用說明

左頁第一個單字。●

KK音標。●

能夠進一步應用已知單字的文法、片語和不規則動詞變化、文化常識等。●

活用單字的例句，依小朋友的吸收能力而寫。●

教育部頒定中小學生必修1200個單字。●

---

am

A

am （我）是；（我）在
[æm]

I am a flower. 我是一朵花。

I am in my room. 我在房間裡。

> am 用於「be 動詞」的現在式第一人稱，詳細內容請參閱第 44 頁。

a.m. 上午 ● p.m.
[ˈeˈɛm]

It's seven a.m. 現在是上午七點。

ambulance 救護車
[ˈæmbjələns]

Teddy calls an ambulance.
泰迪叫了一輛救護車。

America 美國
[əˈmɛrɪkə]

My grandmother lives in America.
我的祖母住在美國。

I am from America.
我來自美國。

本字典包含了教育部頒定國中小學生必備1200個單字，總共收錄約1500個單字。只要能活用本字典中的單字，我們的孩子就算到了國高中，英文能力依然能專美於他人之前。

本字典是以英文字母排列，標以KK發音，其中並沒有繁雜的名詞、形容詞、副詞等詞類標示，以避免造成小朋友在學習上的混亂。小朋友會隨著不斷學習的經驗，自然體會這些詞類的用法。

每一個章節裡都有圖片情境解釋，幫助小朋友更容易記憶英文單字。另外，單字的例句是為了加強小朋友的學習能力而設計，以日常生活為中心編輯而成。期待本字典能夠幫助各位小朋友，建立好紮實的英文基礎。

● 右頁最後一個單字。

● 為強化搜尋功能，將英文字母標示於頁緣。

● 相似詞⊜，相反詞☻

●「百聞不如一見」，聽一百遍單字，不如看一眼圖片，學習效果更顯著。單字搭配圖片，記憶更容易。

animal

A

＊**among** 在…之中；在…中間
[əˈmʌŋ]

Suzzie is sitting among the boys.
蘇西坐在一群男孩中間。

＊**and** 和，跟
[ænd]

I like cake and ice cream.
我喜歡蛋糕和冰淇淋。

angel 天使；守護者 ☻ devil
[ˈændʒl]

Suzzie is an angel to me.
蘇西對我來說是天使。

＊**angry** 生氣的
[ˈæŋgrɪ]

I am angry with you. 我在生你的氣。

＊**animal** 動物
[ˈænəml]

I like cats best among the animals.
在所有動物中我最喜歡貓咪。

29

本書四大輔助記憶特點

四大記憶法 單字過目不忘

特點 ❶ 圖像式記憶

日常生活中普遍使用得到的名詞、形容詞、代名詞、介系詞等單字，這裡用容易理解又有趣的插圖呈現，從圖像建立起孩子的認字能力。

特點 ❷ 情境式記憶

28篇貼近兒童生活範圍的全彩情境圖，運用「情境記憶」模式輕鬆記住500個單字，使孩子能夠具體掌握各種事物的英文名稱，培養孩子的辨析能力。

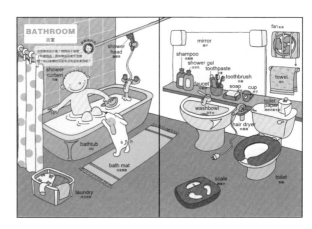

特點 ❸ 聯想式記憶

精心挑選出800個最容易學又一定要會的單字，運用「重複記憶」及「聯想記憶」模式反覆出現在內文的例句與情境圖中，加強孩子對單字的熟悉度，訓練孩子的聯想能力。

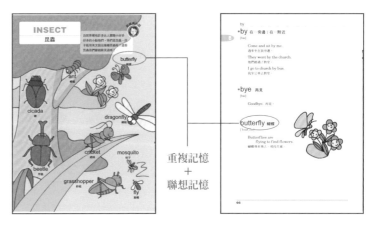

重複記憶
＋
聯想記憶

好厲害!!除了可供查詢,
連字典也可以輕鬆背起來。

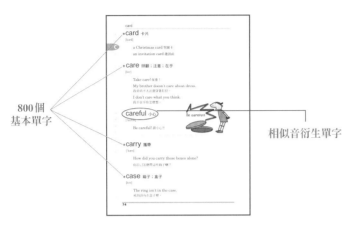

800個
基本單字

相似音衍生單字

特點 ❹ 相似字、音記憶
運用「相似字、相似音記憶」模式,從這800個基本單字中再衍生出200個單字群組,將1000個單字從A到Z按順序排列。

例句中的相關單字,會重複出現在不同例句或情境圖中,特別難的單字會以圖解方式讓孩子自然而然地學習,鞏固孩子的拼字能力。

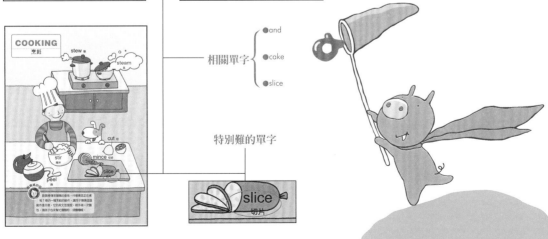

相關單字
- and
- cake
- slice

特別難的單字

目次

超好記!! 發音口訣規則

母音	音標 單字	長短音	發音口訣	有聲	無聲
A	[æ] cat	短音	A小妹沒禮貌，說起話來 [æ] [æ] [æ]	○	
	[ɛ] air	短音	A小妹說笑話，空氣真冷ㄟ [ɛ] [ɛ] [ɛ]	○	
	[ə] about	短音	A小妹大約在這個時候餓了 [ə] [ə] [ə]	○	
	[ɔ] ball	短音	A小妹球打到人了ㄛ! [ɔ] [ɔ] [ɔ]	○	
	[ɑ] far	長音	A小妹的家好遠ㄚ! [ɑ] [ɑ] [ɑ]	○	
	[e] name	長音	A小妹的名字叫做A[e] [e] [e]	○	
B	[b] bye		B小弟說ㄅㄞ、ㄅㄞ [b] [b] [b]	○	
C	[k] car		吃維他命C，不會咳嗽 [k] [k] [k]		×
	[s] bicycle		C小弟髒ㄙㄙ，笑死人 [s] [s] [s]		×
	[tʃ] chair		小麻雀，雀雀雀 [tʃ] [tʃ] [tʃ]	○	
D	[d] dog		你的，我的 [d] [d] [d]	○	
E	[ɛ] bed	短音	E媽媽是ㄟ阿凍瓜 [ɛ] [ɛ] [ɛ]	○	
	[i] bee	長音	兩個E媽媽跑第一 [i] [i] [i]	○	
	[i] sea	長音	E媽和A媽也跑第一 [i] [i] [i]	○	
	[ɚ] mother	長音	E媽和R小妹想吐，嗯嗯嗯 [ɚ] [ɚ] [ɚ]	○	
F	[f] fox		皮ㄈㄨ的 ㄈㄨ [f] [f] [f]		×
G	[g] goat		G小弟割繩子，割割割 [g] [g] [g]	○	
	[dʒ] giraffe		G小弟擠牛奶，擠擠擠 [dʒ] [dʒ] [dʒ]	○	
H	[h] hot		喝水的ㄏ [h] [h] [h]		×
I	[ɪ] pig	短音	1 1 1 [ɪ] [ɪ] [ɪ]	○	
	[aɪ] kite	長音	哎哎哎 [aɪ] [aɪ] [aɪ]	○	
	[ɝ] bird	長音	小鳥兒 [ɝ] [ɝ] [ɝ]	○	
J	[dʒ] jet, cage		擠牛奶，擠擠擠 [dʒ] [dʒ] [dʒ]	○	
K	[k] key		咳嗽的咳 [k] [k] [k]		×
L	[l] leg, tool		打雷ㄌ，ㄌㄌㄌ [l] [l] [l]	○	
M	[m] man, ham		為什麼？為什麼？麼麼麼 [m] [m] [m]	○	
N	[n] not, fan		你的呢？我的呢？呢呢呢 [n] [n] [n]	○	
	[ŋ] sing		你的嗎？我的嗎？嗯嗯嗯 [ŋ] [ŋ] [ŋ]	○	

紅字表示母音
綠字表示子音

母音		音標	單字	長短音	發音口訣	有聲	無聲
O		[ɑ] box		短音	阿婆的ㄚ，阿阿阿 [ɑ][ɑ][ɑ]	○	
		[o] ocean		長音	海鷗的ㄡ，[o][o][o]	○	
		[ɔ] dog		短音	好油ㄛ，[ɔ][ɔ][ɔ]	○	
		[ə] o'clock		短音	七點了，好餓喔 [ə][ə][ə]	○	
		[ʌ] other		短音	阿婆的ㄚ（嘴不要張大）[ʌ][ʌ][ʌ]	○	
		[au] cow		長音	狼叫聲ㄚㄨ [au][au][au]	○	
		[ɔɪ] boy		長音	救護車叫聲ㄛㄧ、ㄛㄧ [ɔɪ][ɔɪ][ɔɪ]	○	
	p	[p] pea			放屁還是放鞭炮，[p][p][p]		×
		[p] puppy			放兩個屁，像在放鞭炮，[p][p][p]		×
	Q	[kw] queen			擴胸擴胸，擴擴擴 [kw][kw][kw]	○	
	R	[r] road			囉囉囉，學老狗叫 [r][r][r]	○	
	S	[s] sun			蛇爬行，嘶嘶嘶 [s][s][s]		×
		[ʒ] usual			雀雀雀（要用喉部發音）[ʒ][ʒ][ʒ]	○	
		[ʃ] ship			噓噓噓 [ʃ][ʃ][ʃ]		×
	T	[t] top			特別的特，[t][t][t]		×
		[θ] think			兩排門牙輕咬舌頭發思音 [θ][θ][θ]		×
		[ð] they			吐舌大喊熱熱熱 [ð][ð][ð]	○	
U		[ʌ] uncle		短音	阿婆的ㄚ（嘴不要張大）[ʌ][ʌ][ʌ]	○	
		[ju] cute		長音	後面有e，前面的u發 [ju]	○	
		[ʊ] put		短音	發短音 [ʊ][ʊ][ʊ]	○	
		[u] pull		長音	發長音 [u][u][u]	○	
	V	[v] vase			勝利的V [v][v][v]	○	
	W	[w] witch			我我我，有口吃；我我我 [w][w][w]	○	
	X	[ks] box			可死可死可死，氣音 [ks][ks][ks]		×
		[z] xylophone			蚊子叫，ㄗㄗㄗ [z][z][z]	○	
	Y	[j] yeah			老爺爺的 [j][j][j]	○	
		[aɪ] fly		長音	鳥會飛，很不賴 [aɪ][aɪ][aɪ]	○	
		[ɪ] happy		短音	快樂的小狗叫黑皮 [ɪ][ɪ][ɪ]	○	
	Z	[z] zebra			蚊子叫，ㄗㄗㄗ [z][z][z]	○	

母音・子音的發音

26 個英文字母中，A、E、I、O、U 這五個字母分別代表五個基本母音發音，其他的字母則為子音發音。一般我們將這些發音分成短母音、長母音、其他母音、半母音、有聲子音和無聲子音。

		有聲子音：	無聲子音：
短母音：	A [æ] [ɛ] [ə] [ɔ] [ɑ] ＊[ɑ]可為長母音或短母音。		
	E [ɛ]	G [g]	K [k]
	I [ɪ]	B [b]	P [p]
	O [ɑ] [ɔ] [ə] [ʌ]	D [d]	T [t]
	U [u] [ʌ]		H [h]
長母音：	A [e] [ɑ] ＊[ɑ]可為長母音或短母音。	V [v]	F [f]
		Z [z]	S [s]
	E [e]　EA [i]　EE [i]	R [r]	
	I [aɪ]	TH [ð]	TH [θ]
	O [o]	S [ʒ]	SH [ʃ]
	U [u]	G [ʤ]	CH [ʧ]
其他母音：	ER [ɚ] [ɝ]	J [ʤ]	
	IR [ɝ]	M [m]	
	OW [aʊ]	N [n]	
	OY [ɔɪ]	NG [ŋ]	
半母音：	Y [j]		
	W [w]		
	L [l]		

短母音

[æ] [ɛ] [ə] [ɔ] [ɑ] [ɪ] [ʊ] [ʌ]

英文中的短母音，有時可單獨發音，有時要和母音或子音合在一起發音。

æ 嘴巴呈扁平狀，發出類似「ㄝ」音。

cat [kæt]（貓）

ɛ 發音類似「ㄝ」，短促音。

desk [dɛsk]（書桌）

ə 嘴巴呈小橢圓形，發出類似「ㄜ」的音，但不捲舌。

Korea [kəˈriə]（韓國）

發音類似「ㄛ」，短促音。

chalk [tʃɔk]（粉筆）

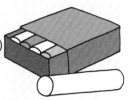

張大嘴巴，發出類似「ㄚ」音。

box [bɑks]（箱子）

嘴形呈扁平狀，發出類似「一」的短促音。

give [gɪv]（給予）

將嘴嘟起，發出類似「ㄨ」的短促音。

look [lʊk]（看）

嘴巴呈大橢圓形，發出介於「ㄚ」和「ㄛ」之間的音。

cup [kʌp]（杯子）

長母音 [ɑ] [e] [i] [aɪ]
[o] [u] [ɚ] [ɝ] [aʊ] [ɔɪ]

張大嘴巴，發出「ㄚ～ㄚ」的長音。 **father** [ˈfɑðɚ]（爸爸）

發音類似「せ～せ」的長音。 **gate** [get]（門）

嘴形呈扁平狀，發出類似「ー～ー」的長音。 **read** [rid]（閱讀）

aI

「ㄚ」發重長音，「一」發輕音，一起發出「ㄚ一」長音。

tiger [ˈtaɪgɚ]

（老虎）

o

略微張大，發出「ㄛ～ㄛ」的長音，同時將舌尖向上捲起。

door [dor]

（門）

u

嘴巴呈嘟嘴狀，發出「ㄨ～ㄨ」的長音。

spoon [spun]

（湯匙）

ɚ

稍微張開嘴巴，發出「ㄛ～ㄛ」長音的同時，要捲起一半的舌尖。

finger [ˈfɪŋgɚ]

（手指）

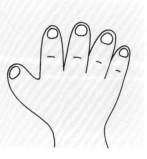

稍微張開嘴巴，發出「ㄜ～ㄜ」長音的同時，要捲起整個舌尖。

girl [gɝl]（女孩）

稍微張開嘴巴，發出「ㄚ～ㄨ」長音。

cow [kau]（乳牛）

稍微張開嘴巴，發出「ㄛ～ㄧ」長音。

boy [bɔɪ]（男孩）

半母音

[j] [w] [l]

j 嘴形呈扁平狀，發出類似「一せ」的短促音。

yawn [jɔn]

（打呵欠）

w 嘴巴呈嘟嘴狀，發出「ㄨ一」的短促音。

watch [watʃ]

（手錶）

l 類似「ㄌ」音。

lily [ˈlɪlɪ] （百合花）

子音

$$[k,g]\ [p,b]\ [t,d]\ [h]\ [f,v]\ [s,z]\ [r]$$
$$[\theta,\eth]\ [\int,\mathfrak{z}]\ [t\int,\mathfrak{d}\mathfrak{z}]\ [m]\ [n]\ [\eta]$$

---

k,g

將舌頭後半部稍微隆起，發類似「ㄎ，ㄍ」音。

kite [kaɪt]
（風箏）

game [gem]
（遊戲）

---

p,b

緊閉嘴唇，瞬間吐氣同時發類似「ㄆ，ㄅ」音。

pen [pɛn]
（筆）

bed [bɛd]
（床）

---

t,d

將舌尖緊貼上牙齒，舌尖彈開時發「ㄊ，ㄉ」音。

doctor [ˈdɑktɚ]
（醫生）

tender [ˈtɛndɚ]
（柔軟的）

h

強烈的喉音，類似「ㄏ」音。

hot [hɑt]

（熱的）

f,v

牙齒輕碰下唇，發類似「ㄈㄨ，ㄈ」音。

foot [fʊt]

（腳）

very [ˈvɛrɪ]

（非常）

s,z

將嘴巴合上，舌尖頂住牙齒，發類似「ㄙ，ㄇ」音。

study [ˈstʌdɪ]

（學習）

zoo [zu]（動物園）

r

舌尖稍微捲起，發類似「ㄖㄜ」音。

bread [brɛd]

（麵包）

θ,ð

嘴巴微張，舌尖頂在上下齒之間，「θ」發類似「ㄙ」音，「ð」發類似「ㄉ」音。

think [θɪŋk]

（想）

they [ðe]（他們）

嘴形呈發出「ㄨ」的樣子，發類似「ㄒㄩ，ㄐㄩ」音。

ship [ʃip]

（船）

u**s**ual [ˈjuʒuəl]

（通常的）

舌尖頂住上牙齦，瞬間彈開時發類似「ㄑㄩ，ㄐㄩ」音。

chur**ch** [tʃɝtʃ]

（教會）

joy [dʒɔɪ]

（歡樂）

嘴巴閉上，發類似「ㄇ」的鼻音。

mat**ch** [mætʃ]

（火柴盒）

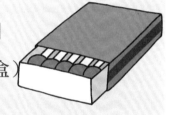

嘴巴微張，舌尖頂住上牙齦，發類似「ㄋ」鼻音。

name [nem]

（名字）

類似「ㄥ」的鼻音。

si**ng** [sɪŋ]

（唱歌）

首先，找一張舒適的沙發或椅子，靠在床頭也可以。

放鬆心情，讓孩子依偎在懷裡。帶著孩子一起唸生字，

生字旁如果有插圖，唸完生字後，

請用生動活潑的語調講解插圖，增進孩子連結圖像與聲音的記憶能力。

*a / an 一個；某個

[ə / æn]

a pretty girl 一個漂亮的女孩　　　I am a boy. 我是一個男生。

an apple tree 一棵蘋果樹

 許多名詞是可數名詞。當這些名詞只有一個的時候，前面要加上 a，但是如果這個名詞是以母音（a、e、i、o、u）開頭，那麼就要在名詞前加上 an。

able 能夠；會 ⊜ can

['ebḷ]

Suzzie is able to play baseball.
蘇西會打棒球。

be able to = can 能夠；會

*about 大概，大約；有關

[ə'baʊt]

It takes about two hours. 這大約要花費兩小時。

a book about animals 一本有關動物的書

above 在上；在…上面

[ə´bʌv]

The plane is flying above the clouds.
這架飛機正飛翔在白雲上。

absent 缺席的 ● present

[´æbsn̩t]

Teddy is absent from school today.
泰迪今天缺席沒來上課。

be absent from 是片語「缺席」的意思。

accident 意外

[´æksədənt]

a car accident 一場車禍

＊across 對面；越過

[ə´krɔs]

Suzzie lives across the river.
蘇西住在河的對面。

＊act 舉動；扮演

[ækt]

Teddy acts like a baby. 泰迪的舉動像小孩一樣。

Suzzie acts Julict. 蘇西扮演茱麗葉。

add 加入
[æd]

Add sugar to coffee, please.
請把糖加入咖啡裡。

★address 地址
[ə'drɛs]

What is your e-mail address?
你的電子郵件地址是什麼？

adult 成熟的；成年人 ⟷ child
[ə'dʌlt]

Adults Only 只限成年人

adventure 冒險
[əd'vɛntʃɚ]

Suzzie likes stories of adventure.
蘇西喜歡冒險故事。

advise 勸告
[əd'vaɪz]

Teddy advised Suzzie to get up early.
泰迪勸告蘇西早點起床。

B
C
D
E
F
G
H
I
J
K
L
M
N
O
P
Q
R
S
T
U
V
W
X
Y
Z

*afraid 害怕的

[ə'fred]

Suzzie is afraid of snakes.
蘇西怕蛇。

be afraid of
是片語「害怕」的意思。

*after 在後；之後；在…之後 ↔ before

['æftə]

Brush your teeth clean after eating sweets.
吃過甜食之後你要把牙齒刷乾淨。

*afternoon 下午

['æftə'nun]

Suzzie will go fishing tomorrow afternoon.
蘇西明天下午要去釣魚。

*again 又；再一次

[ə'gɛn]

Teddy cries again. 泰迪又哭了。

*age 年齡，年紀

[edʒ]

We are of the same age. 我們年齡一樣大。

*ago 以前
[ə´go]

I saw you two days ago. 我兩天前看過你。

agree 同意；一致 ⊙ disagree
[ə´gri]

I agree with you. 我和你意見一致。

ahead 向前
[ə´hɛd]

Go straight ahead. 向前直走。

*air 空氣
[ɛr]

We can't live without air.
沒有空氣，我們無法生存。

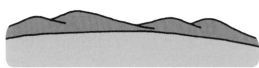

airplane / plane 飛機
[´ɛr͵plen / plen]

We went to Japan by airplane. 我們坐飛機去了日本。

*airport 機場
[´ɛr͵port]

We picked up our aunt at the airport.
我們在機場接阿姨回家。

*album 相簿；唱片

[ˈælbəm]

Can I see your photo album?
我可以看你的相簿嗎？

alarm 警報；鬧鐘

[əˈlɑrm]

a fire alarm 一場火警

I set the alarm for seven. 我將鬧鐘設在七點鐘。

alive 活生生的 ⊙ dead

[əˈlaɪv]

Teddy catches dragonflies alive.
泰迪捉到活的蜻蜓。

*all 全部，都

[ɔl]

We are all happy.
我們全都很快樂。

allowance 零用錢；津貼

[əˈlaʊəns]

Give me my allowance. 給我零用錢。

alone 孤獨，一個人 ⇄ together

[ə'lon]

Suzzie stayed at home alone today.
蘇西今天一個人在家。

✱along 沿著

[ə'lɔŋ]

Let's go along the river. 讓我們沿著河走。

aloud 大聲地

[ə'laud]

Read aloud, please.
請大聲地唸出來。

also 也；而且 ⊖ too

['ɔlso]

Teddy is also eating chocolate.
泰迪也在吃巧克力。

Suzzie also speaks German.
蘇西也會說德國話。

✱always 總是

['ɔlwez]

Teddy is always late for school. 泰迪上學總是遲到。

am （我）是；（我）在
[æm]

I am a flower. 我是一朵花。

I am in my room. 我在房間裡。

> am 用於「be 動詞」的現在式第一人稱，詳細內容請參閱第 44 頁。

a.m. 上午 ⬌ p.m.
[ˈeˈem]

It's seven a.m. 現在是上午七點。

ambulance 救護車
[ˈæmbjələns]

Teddy calls an ambulance.
泰迪叫了一輛救護車。

America 美國
[əˈmɛrɪkə]

My grandmother lives in America.
我的祖母住在美國。

I am from America.
我來自美國。

*among 在…之中；在…中間

[ə'mʌŋ]

Suzzie is sitting among the boys.
蘇西坐在一群男孩中間。

*and 和，跟

[ænd]

I like cake and ice cream.
我喜歡蛋糕和冰淇淋。

angel 天使；守護者 ⊖ devil

['ændʒl]

Suzzie is an angel to me.
蘇西對我來說是天使。

*angry 生氣的

['æŋgrɪ]

I am angry with you. 我在生你的氣。

*animal 動物

['ænəml]

I like cats best among the animals.
在所有動物中我最喜歡貓咪。

another 另一個；再一個

[əˈnʌðɚ]

Tell me another story! 告訴我另一個故事吧！

Show me another dress, please. 請給我看另一件套裝。

*answer 回答；允諾 ⬥ ask

[ˈænsɚ]

Answer me this question. 回答我這個問題。

ant 螞蟻

[ænt]

Ants like sweets.
螞蟻喜歡甜食。

*any 任何

[ˈɛnɪ]

Choose any dress you like. 選擇任何你喜歡的衣服。

Do you have any money? 你有任何錢嗎？

anyone 每一個（人）；任何一個（人）

[ˈɛnɪˌwʌn]

Anyone can do it!
每一個人都能做到！

Can anyone answer my question?
有任何人可以回答我的問題嗎？

anything 任何事

[ˈɛnɪˌθɪŋ]

I will do anything for you. 我願為你做任何事。

★apartment 公寓

[əˈpɑrtmənt]

My apartment has many rooms.
我的公寓有很多房間。

★apple 蘋果

[ˈæpl̩]

We can get apples in autumn.
我們可以在秋天時採蘋果。

April 四月

[ˈeprəl]

In April, Suzzie plants trees.
蘇西在四月時種樹。

apron 圍裙

[ˈeprən]

Apron keeps your clothes clean.
圍裙讓你的衣服保持清潔。

are （你／你們）是；（你／你們）在
[ɑr]

You are a genius. 你是一個天才。

Teddy and Suzzie are in the kitchen.
泰迪跟蘇西在廚房。

 主詞若是複數（一個以上）名詞，或是 "you" 的時候，後面的動詞若是「是」或「在」的意思，則要用 be 動詞現在式第二人稱 are 來表示。

✽**arm** 手臂
[ɑrm]

My arms are longer than you.
我的手臂比你長。

✽**around** 圍著，圍繞
[ə'raʊnd]

We sat around the fire. 我們圍著營火坐下。

Teddy travels around the country. 泰迪在這個國家旅行。

✽**arrive** 抵達；送達 ➡ leave
[ə'raɪv]

We arrived in New York yesterday. 我們昨天抵達紐約。

The letter arrived this morning. 這封信今早送達。

A

art 藝術

[ɑrt]

Art is long, life is short.
藝術是長久的，生命是短暫的。

My favorite subject is art.
我最喜歡的科目是美術。

★as 如同…一樣

[əs]

Teddy runs as fast as you.
泰迪跑起來跟你一樣快。

Asia 亞洲

[ˈeʃə]

There are many countries in Asia.
在亞洲有許多國家。

★ask 詢問 ⟷ answer

[æsk]

Don't ask me such a difficult question.
不要問我這麼難的問題。

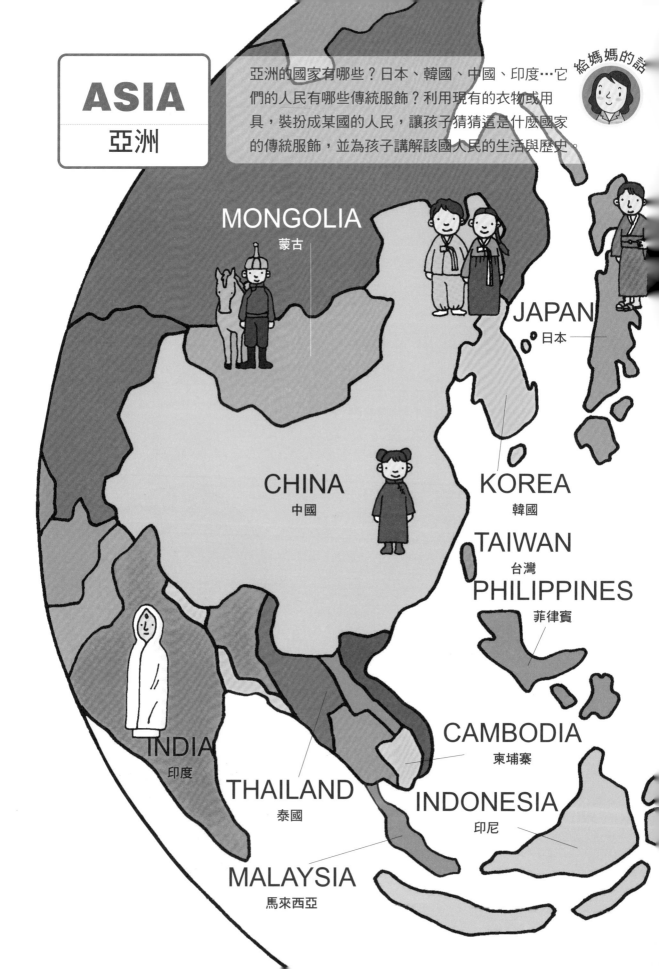

ASIA
亞洲

亞洲的國家有哪些？日本、韓國、中國、印度⋯它們的人民有哪些傳統服飾？利用現有的衣物或用具，裝扮成某國的人民，讓孩子猜猜這是什麼國家的傳統服飾，並為孩子講解該國人民的生活與歷史。

給媽媽的話

MONGOLIA
蒙古

JAPAN
日本

KOREA
韓國

CHINA
中國

TAIWAN
台灣

PHILIPPINES
菲律賓

INDIA
印度

CAMBODIA
柬埔寨

THAILAND
泰國

INDONESIA
印尼

MALAYSIA
馬來西亞

asleep 睡著的，入睡的

[ə´slip]

Everyone falls asleep in the palace.
皇宮裡每一個人都安然入睡。

*at 在

[æt]

Let's meet at the station. 我們約在火車站碰面吧。

I went to bed at ten o'clock yesterday.
我昨天十點上床睡覺。

attention 注意，留心

[ə´tɛnʃən]

Attention, please! 請注意！

August 八月

[´ɔgəst]

I was born in August.
我在八月出生。

✱aunt 阿姨；舅媽；姑姑；伯母 ⊖ uncle
[ænt]

I live with my aunt. 我跟阿姨一起住。

aunt 是對女方親戚長輩的統稱。所以，依當時的情況可解釋為阿姨、舅媽、姑姑或伯母等稱謂。

automobile / auto 汽車
[ˈɔtəməˌbɪl]

Today, many people have automobiles.
在今天，很多人都有汽車。

✱autumn 秋天 ⊖ fall
[ˈɔtɚm]

Many leaves are fallen in autumn.
許多樹葉到了秋天都會凋落。

9 September
10 October
11 November

✱away 離開；（公里、英哩等距離）遠
[əˈwe]

Don't go away. 不要離開。

It is six miles away. 有六英哩遠。

Write the missing letters
空格中填入適當的字母

給媽媽的話

帶著孩子一起做練習，先看看孩子唸不唸得出對應圖片的生字，並將空格填滿。如果孩子唸不出，再唸給孩子聽。

al☐rm

ang☐l

app☐e

☐nt

☐mbul☐nce

alarm, angel, apple,
ant, ambulance

給媽媽的話

首先，找一張舒適的沙發或椅子，靠在床頭也可以。
放鬆心情，讓孩子依偎在懷裡。帶著孩子一起唸生字，
生字旁如果有插圖，唸完生字後，
請用生動活潑的語調講解插圖，增進孩子連結圖像與聲音的記憶能力。

B b [bi]

★ baby 嬰兒；寶貝
['bebɪ]

A baby is sleeping. 寶寶正在睡覺。

★ back 後面；背後 ↔ front
[bæk]

Is there something on my back?
有東西在我背後嗎？

★ bad 壞的；糟的
[bæd]

a bad tooth 一顆壞牙

I feel bad this morning.
我今天早上感到很糟。

*bag 袋子

[bæg]

You have to buy a plastic bag.
你必須買一個塑膠袋。

在美國，人們稱呼塑膠袋叫做 plastic bag，
並沒有特別的專有名詞。

*ball 球

[bɔl]

I lost my ball. 我的球不見了。

I found your ball on the roof.
我發現你的球在屋頂上。

*balloon 氣球

[bəˊlun]

Blow up this balloon, please. 請吹這個氣球。

*banana 香蕉

[bəˊnænə]

Teddy eats a banana every morning.
泰迪每天早上吃一根香蕉。

*band 樂團；帶子；細繩

[bænd]

a rubber band 一條橡皮筋

a jazz band 一個爵士樂團

*bank 銀行

[bæŋk]

Why did you rob the bank?
你為什麼要搶銀行？

*base 基礎；出發點

[bes]

a baseline 底線

This is based on the same rule.
這是基於同樣的法則。

*basket 籃子

['bæskɪt]

I put my dog in the basket whenever I go out.
只要我外出，我就把狗狗放進籃子裡。

bat 蝙蝠；棒子

[bæt]

Where is my baseball bat? 我的球棒在哪裡？

I saw many bats in the cave. 我看到許多蝙蝠在山洞裡。

*bath 洗澡，沐浴

[bæθ]

I am going to take a bath, first.
我要先去洗個澡。

BATHROOM
浴室

給媽媽的話

浴室裡有些什麼？問問孩子發現
了什麼物品，那件物品的英文怎麼
說。自己家裡的浴室有沒有這些東西呢？

shower
head
蓮蓬頭

shower
curtain
浴簾

bathtub
浴缸

bath mat
浴室踏墊

laundry
待洗衣物

⭐be

[bi]

「be 動詞」是中文「是，在」的意思。

舉例來說，句子 I   am   a gril （我是小女孩）裡，
            我   是   小女孩

「am」為「是」的意思。

「be動詞」會隨主詞（I，you，he，she，it）和時空（現在式，過
去式）而改變。有些複雜是嗎？在這裡，只要先知道 be 動詞是什
麼就可以了。

隨人稱而不同的 be 動詞變化

時 態	人 稱	單 數	複 數
現在式	第一人稱	I **am**	we **are**
	第二人稱	you **are**	you **are**
	第三人稱	he she **is** it	they **are**
過去式	第一人稱	I **was**	we **were**
	第二人稱	you **were**	you **were**
	第三人稱	he she **was** it	they **were**

⋆beach 海灘，海濱

[bitʃ]

We played in the beach all day.
我們整天在海灘上玩。

bean 豆子

[bin]

What kind of beans can't we grow in a garden?
我們不能在花園裡種哪種豆子？

I hate eating beans.
我討厭吃豆子。

⋆bear 熊

[bɛr]

a black bear 一隻黑熊

a polar bear 一隻北極熊

⋆beautiful 漂亮的，美麗的

[ˈbjutəfəl]

This poem is really beautiful.
這首詩真美。

⋆because 因為

[bɪˈkɔz]

I couldn't sleep last night
because of a mosquito.
因為一隻蚊子，我昨天晚上睡不著。

BEACH
海灘

water skiing
滑水

swimming tube
游泳圈

yacht
帆船

swimsuit
泳裝

hermit crab
寄居蟹

crab
螃蟹

beach umbrella
海灘遮陽傘

starfish
海星

conch
海螺

sunglasses
太陽眼鏡

*become 變成；變得

[bɪˋkʌm]

We become famous. 我們變得有名。

*bed 床

[bɛd]

Don't hop on the bed. 不要在床上跳。

It's time for bed. 上床時間到了。

bedroom 臥室

[ˋbɛdˌrum]

Your bedroom is really wonderful.
你的臥室真是漂亮。

bee 蜜蜂

[bi]

The bees will not sting.
這種蜜蜂不會刺人。

beef 牛肉

[bif]

Some people don't eat beef.
有些人不吃牛肉。

✱before 在前；之前；在…之前；在…面前

[brˈfor]

I have seen that film before. 我之前已經看過那部片子。

Teddy stood before the President. 泰迪站在總統面前。

✱begin 開始

[brˈgɪn]

The meeting will begin at eight. 會議將在八點開始。

It began to snow. 開始下雪了。

✱behind 在後；在…背後

[brˈhaɪnd]

What is it you are hiding behind you?
你藏在背後的是什麼？

✱bell 鈴；鈴聲

[bɛl]

Why do cows have bells on their necks?
為什麼乳牛都有鈴噹在脖子上？

✱below 在下；在…下面

[bəˈlo]

Just fill in the form below, please.
請填寫下面的表格。

BEDROOM
臥室

desk lamp
檯燈

curtain
窗簾

book
書

desk
桌子

chair
椅

trash can
垃圾桶

soccer ball
足球

toy
玩具

popcorn
爆米花

TOY

fish globe
魚缸

goldfish
金魚

card
紙牌

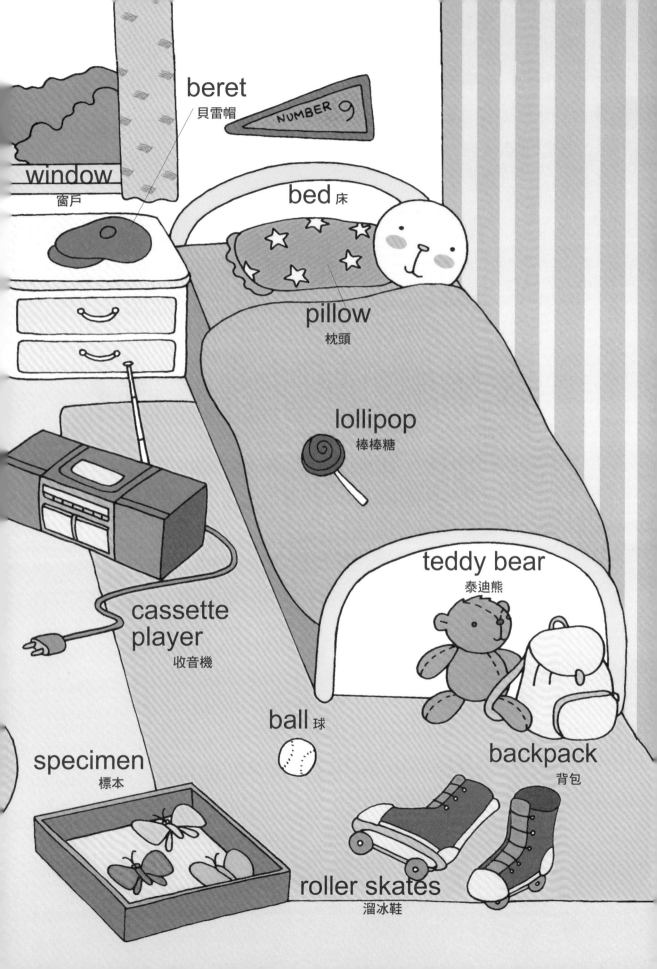

belt 皮帶，腰帶

[bɛlt]

I don't need a belt.
我不需要皮帶。

*bench 板凳

[bɛntʃ]

The bench was wet.
這張板凳濕濕的。

*beside 在…旁邊

[bɪ'saɪd]

Suzzie sat beside me. 蘇西坐在我旁邊。

best 最佳的，最好的 ⊝ worst

[bɛst]

I work best early in the morning.
我一大早時工作狀態最好。

Who did it best? 誰做得最好？

*between 兩者之間；在…中間
[bɪˈtwin]

A butterfly is flying between flowers.
一隻蝴蝶在花叢中飛舞。

There is no secret between you and me.
你我之間沒有祕密。

*bicycle / bike 腳踏車
[ˈbaɪsɪkl̩ / baɪk]

I like to ride a bicycle.
我喜歡騎腳踏車。

Suzzie goes to school on her bicycle.
蘇西騎腳踏車上學。

*big 大的 ↔ little, small
[bɪg]

Teddy is big for his age. 泰迪這樣的年紀算是大塊頭。

*bird 小鳥
[bɝd]

The early bird catches the worm.
早起的鳥兒有蟲吃。

BIRD
鳥類

早起的鳥兒有蟲吃。樹上有哪些鳥兒？陸地上有哪些鳥兒？水裡又有哪些鳥兒？看看孩子能否將牠們的英文說出來。可以的話，試著模仿鳥兒的叫聲，會更有趣喔。

給媽媽的話

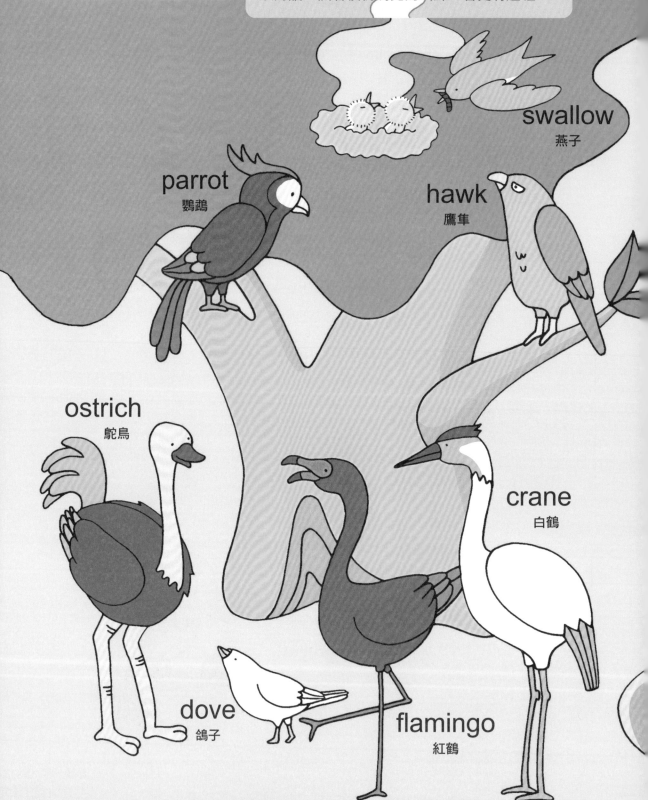

swallow
燕子

parrot
鸚鵡

hawk
鷹隼

ostrich
鴕鳥

crane
白鶴

dove
鴿子

flamingo
紅鶴

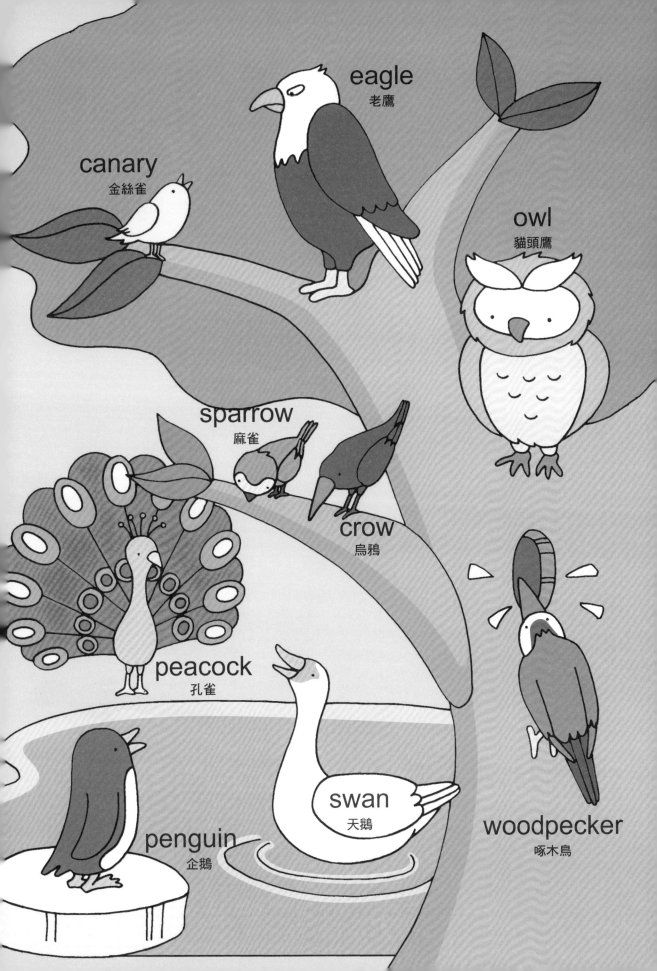

★birthday 生日

[ˈbɝθˌde]

When is your birthday?
你的生日是什麼時候？

Happy birthday to you.
祝你生日快樂。

bite 咬（傷）；咬住

[baɪt]

My dog never bites. 我的狗從不咬人。

Teddy bit off a piece of cake.
泰迪咬了一口蛋糕。

★black 黑色；黑色的

[blæk]

My mother has many black dresses.
我媽媽有許多黑色洋裝。

Black shadow follows me.
黑影跟隨著我。

blanket 毛毯

[ˈblæŋkɪt]

Mother pulled the blanket over me.
媽媽鋪那張毛毯在我身上。

*blow 吹拂，吹過

[blo]

It is blowing hard.
現在風很大。

Don't blow your breath on my face.
不要在我臉上吹氣。

*blue 藍色；藍色的；憂鬱的

[blu]

Your eyes are blue.
你的眼睛是藍色的。

Why is the sky blue?
為什麼天空是藍色的？

*board 佈告欄；黑板

[bord]

The papers were pinned up on the board.
那些報紙被釘在佈告欄上。

Write your full name on the board.
在黑板上寫下你的全名。

*boat 船

[bot]

How do boats float? 船如何能浮起來？

BODY
身體

"**Head, shoulders, knees and toes / Knees and toes / Knees and toes / …**" 教孩子唱這首與身體部位有關的英文兒歌，能夠邊唱歌邊做體操那就更好囉。

給媽媽的話

head
頭

face
臉

neck
脖子

elbow
手肘

finger
手指

knee
膝蓋

heel
腳踝

toe
腳趾

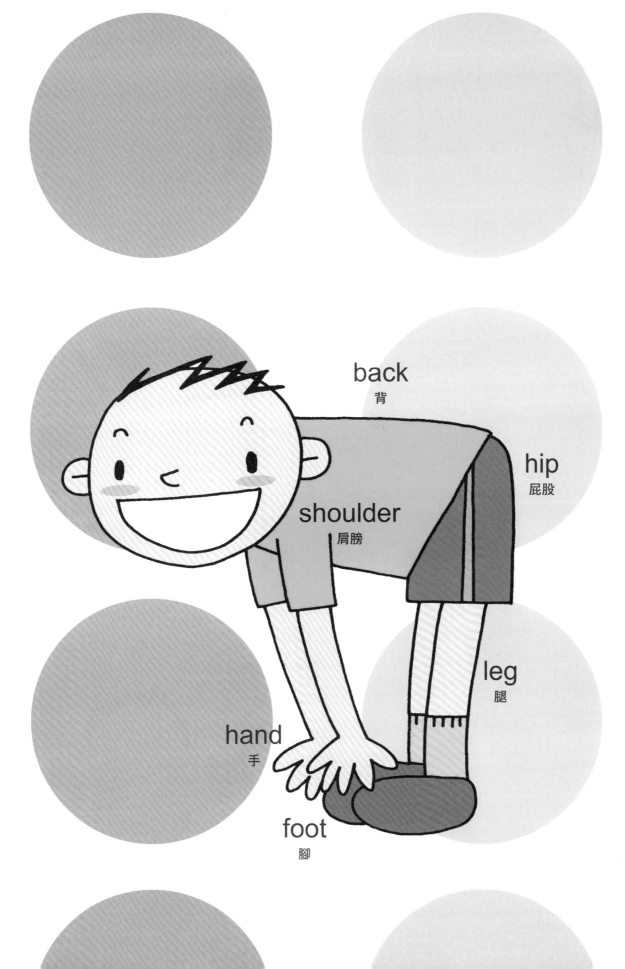

＊body 身體

[ˈbɑdɪ]

A sound mind is in a sound body.
健全的心靈存在於健康的身體之中。

＊book 書本

[bʊk]

I read books quickly.
我讀書的速度很快。

I don't like a thick book.
我不喜歡厚厚的書。

boot 靴子

[but]

There are stones in my boots. 我的靴子裡有石頭。

borrow 借

[ˈbɑro]

Can I borrow that book? 我能借那本書嗎？

both 兩者

[boθ]

I don't want both books.
這兩本書我都不想要。

Mom loves both of you.
媽媽愛你們兩個人。

*bottle 瓶子

[ˈbɑtl̩]

Shake the bottles before you drink it.
在喝飲料之前搖一搖瓶子。

*bowl 碗

[bol]

I need a bowl instead of cups. 我需要一個碗而不是杯子。

*box 箱子

[bɑks]

There was a cat in the box.
箱子裡有一隻貓。

Open the box. 打開這個箱子。

*boy 男孩

[bɔɪ]

You are a bright boy. 你是一個聰明的男孩。

*bread 麵包；食物

[brɛd]

Who made this bread? 誰做了這個麵包？

It is time to bake bread in the oven.
該是將麵包送進烤箱烘烤的時候了。

*break 打破；破裂

[brek]

My little sister broke a cup in two.
我妹妹把一個杯子打破成了兩半。

Who broke the window?
誰打破了窗戶？

break 的過去式是 broke，過去分詞是 broken，有一點難哦。現在只要知道在描述過去的事情時，動詞會有不同的寫法就可以了。

*breakfast 早餐

[ˈbrɛkfəst]

At what time do you have breakfast?
你都幾點吃早餐？

I like egg and toast for breakfast.
早餐我喜歡吃蛋跟吐司。

那麼，午餐和晚餐怎麼說呢？午餐是 lunch，晚餐是 supper。另外，一天中最盛重的一餐叫做 dinner。

*bridge 橋

[brɪdʒ]

They build a bridge over a river.
他們在河上搭建一座橋。

We saw a rainbow on the bridge.
我們在橋上看見一道彩虹。

★bright 明亮的

[braɪt]

The moon is bright. 月亮很明亮。

Suzzie shows us a bright smile.
蘇西給我們一個燦爛的笑容。

★bring 攜帶；帶來

[brɪŋ]

Bring me some flowers. 帶給我一些花。

I didn't bring my umbrella. 我沒有帶傘來。

★brother 兄弟

[ˈbrʌðɚ]

Say hello to your brother.
向你的兄弟問好。

★brown 棕色；棕色的

[braʊn]

I dyed my hair brown. 我把頭髮染成棕色

★brush 刷洗；刷子

[brʌʃ]

Brush your teeth clean before you go to bed.
睡覺前牙要刷乾淨。

I brushed the dust from my father's shoes.
我幫爸爸的鞋子刷去灰塵。

＊build 搭建，建造

[bɪld]

My grandfather has built me a little cabin on the tree.
我的祖父已經為我蓋了一間樹屋。

They are building a school.
他們正在興建一所學校。

> build 過去式和過去分詞都是 built。另外，building 是「建築物」的統稱。

＊burn 燃燒；燒焦

[bɝn]

The meat is burning. 肉快要燒焦了。

> burn 過去式和過去分詞可以是 burned 或 burnt，詳細內容請待下回分解。

＊bus 公車；巴士

[bʌs]

What bus do I take to get to the zoo?
我可以搭哪一台巴士到動物園？

I go to school by bus.
我搭公車上學。

*busy 忙碌的

['bɪzɪ]

Teddy is busy at his desk preparing for the exam.
泰迪正在書桌前忙著準備考試。

*but 但是，不過

[bʌt]

Teddy is poor but cheerful. 泰迪雖然貧窮卻很樂觀。

Teddy didn't go, but Suzzie did.
泰迪沒有去，不過蘇西去了。

*butter 奶油

['bʌtɚ]

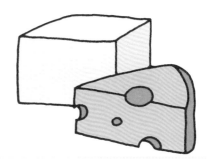

peanut butter 花生醬

*button 按鈕；鈕釦

['bʌtn̩]

I missed a button. 我掉了一顆鈕釦。

Press a button to open the door. 按下按鈕就可以開門。

*buy 購買，買入

[baɪ]

Buy me that doll.
幫我買那個洋娃娃。

I want to buy a violin.
我想買一台小提琴。

★by 在…旁邊；在…附近
[baɪ]

Come and sit by me.
過來坐在我旁邊。

They went by the church.
他們經過了教堂。

I go to church by bus.
我坐公車去教堂。

★bye 再見
[baɪ]

Goodbye. 再見。

butterfly 蝴蝶
[ˈbʌtɚˌflaɪ]

Butterflies are
flying to find flowers.
蝴蝶飛來飛去，尋找花蜜。

Write the missing letters

空格中填入適當的字母

給媽媽的話

帶著孩子一起做練習，先看看孩子唸不唸得出對應圖片的生字，並將空格填滿。如果孩子唸不出，再唸給孩子聽。

bo☐k

bot☐le

☐irth☐ay

☐us

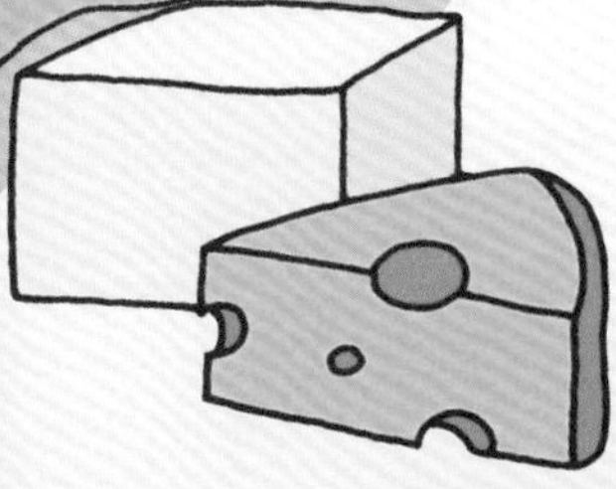

but☐er

bottle, book,
birthday, bus, butter

給媽媽的話

首先，找一張舒適的沙發或椅子，靠在床頭也可以。
放鬆心情，讓孩子依偎在懷裡。帶著孩子一起唸生字，
生字旁如果有插圖，唸完生字後，
請用生動活潑的語調講解插圖，增進孩子連結圖像與聲音的記憶能力。

[si]

cabbage 包心菜，甘藍菜

['kæbɪʤ]

Do rabbits eat cabbage?
兔子吃包心菜嗎？

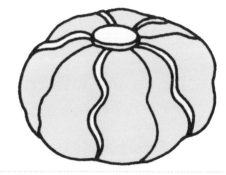

＊cake 蛋糕

[kek]

Let's slice the cake in two.
我們把蛋糕切成兩塊吧。

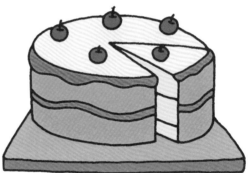

＊calendar 日曆

['kæləndɚ]

A calendar is hung on the wall.
一本日曆掛在牆上。

✳ call 呼叫；稱呼

[kɔl]

Just call me Suzzie. 就叫我蘇西吧。

Would you call me at seven? 你能在七點時叫醒我嗎？

✳ camera 照相機

[ˈkæmərə]

I want to buy a new camera. 我想買一架新的相機。

✳ camp 營地；駐紮處

[kæmp]

Let's camp out in the woods.
我們在樹林裡搭帳篷吧。

✳ can 能夠；會

[kæn]

Can you swim? 你會游泳嗎？ Yes, I can. 是的，我會。

Suzzie can play the violin. 蘇西會拉小提琴。

I can do it. 我可以做這件事。

✳ candle 蠟燭

[ˈkændl̩]

A candle is burning. 一支蠟燭正在燃燒。

✱ candy 糖果

[ˈkændɪ]

Teddy is fond of candy.
泰迪喜歡吃糖果。

✱ cap 帽子

[kæp]

My father is wearing a baseball cap.
我爸爸戴著一頂棒球帽。

✱ capital 首都

[ˈkæpət!]

Seoul is the capital of Korea. 首爾是韓國的首都。

✱ captain 機長；艦長；隊長

[ˈkæptɪn]

My father is a captain.
我的爸爸是艦長。

I am the captain of this team.

我是這一隊的隊長。

✱ car 汽車

[kɑr]

My dog is in the car alone.
我的小狗獨自待在汽車裡面。

steam engine
蒸汽火車

super express
高速火車

dump truck 傾卸車

bulldozer 推土機

automobile
汽車

crane
起重機，吊車

tram 有軌電車

motorcycle
摩托車

CAR
車子

train 火車

taxi 計程車

bus 公車

patrol car 巡邏警車

garbage truck 垃圾車

ambulance 救護車

fire engine 消防車

racing car 賽車

⚹card 卡片

[kɑrd]

a Christmas card 一張聖誕卡

an invitation card 一封邀請函

⚹care 照顧；注意；在乎

[kɛr]

Take care! 保重！

My brother doesn't care about dress.
我弟弟不太注意穿著打扮。

I don't care what you think.
我不在乎你怎麼想。

careful 小心的

[ˈkɛrfəl]

Be careful! 請小心！！

Be careful!

⚹carry 攜帶

[ˈkærɪ]

How did you carry these boxes alone?

你自己怎麼帶這些箱子啊？

⚹case 箱子；盒子

[kes]

The ring isn't in the case.
戒指沒有在盒子裡。

✱cassette 錄音帶

[kə′sɛt]

I need cassette tapes. 我需要錄音帶。

✱cat 貓

[kæt]

I will give you a cat.
我將送你一隻貓。

✱catch 逮捕；牽著

[kætʃ]

The policeman catches a thief.
警察抓到一個小偷。

Mother catches me by the hand.
媽媽牽著我的手。

✱ceiling 天花板

[′silɪŋ]

Can you touch the ceiling? 你能摸到天花板嗎？

✱center 中心，中央

[′sɛntɚ]

There is a piano in the center of the cafe.
這間咖啡廳的中間有一架鋼琴。

the center of a town 小鎮的中心

*chair 椅子

[tʃɛr]

The book is on the chair.
這本書在椅子上。

*chalk 粉筆

[tʃɔk]

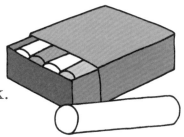

Mark the door with a yellow chalk.
在門上用黃色粉筆做記號。

*chance 機會

[tʃæns]

It is a good chance for me to go abroad.
這是我出國的好機會。

*change 改變；變動

[tʃendʒ]

a change of seasons 季節的變換

I changed my mind. 我改變心意了。

*cheap 便宜的 ⟷ expensive

[tʃip]

The price is very cheap. 這個價格非常便宜。

Teddy sells cheap candies. 泰迪在賣便宜的糖果。

check 檢查

[tʃɛk]

Check the answers. 檢查這些答案。

cheek 臉頰

[tʃik]

Suzzie has rosy cheeks. 蘇西有紅通通的臉頰。

My mother kissed me on my cheek.
我媽媽親我的臉頰。

★cheese 乳酪，起司

[tʃiz]

Say cheese. 把嘴張開成說「起司」的樣子。
（幫人拍照時的用語）

chest 胸腔，胸膛

[tʃɛst]

There is a medal on his chest.
他的胸前戴著一面獎牌。

★chicken 雞肉

[´tʃɪkɪn]

Let's have chicken for dinner. 我們晚餐吃雞肉吧。

CLASSROOM
教室

clock 鐘

bell 響鈴

calendar 日曆

board 佈告欄

map 地圖

咚—咚—咚—咚—，上課啦。孩子記不記得學校的教室裡有哪些東西呢？要能說出它們的英文喔。給孩子一盒蠟筆及許多廢紙，由家長做老師，說出一樣東西的英文，請孩子將它畫出來。如果孩子只是想盡情塗鴉，也不要阻止，但別忘了問孩子畫的是什麼。

pencil sharpener 削鉛筆機

eraser 橡皮擦

pencil box 鉛筆盒

pencil 鉛筆

desk 桌子

chair 椅子

給媽媽的話

∗child 孩童，兒童 children

[tʃaɪld]

Any child knows it. 每個孩子都知道這件事。

He is only a child. 他不過是個孩子。

複數（有兩個以上的孩子）時，不能說 childs，正確的說法是 children [ˈtʃɪldrən]。

chimney 煙囪

[ˈtʃɪmnɪ]

Keep your chimney clean.
保持你家的煙囪暢通乾淨。

chin 下巴

[tʃɪn]

He hit me on the chin. 他撞到了我的下巴。

∗chopsticks 筷子

[ˈtʃɑpˌstɪks]

Use your chopsticks instead of forks.
用你的筷子而不是叉子。

∗church 教堂；教會

[tʃɝtʃ]

We go to church every Sunday.
每個星期日我們都會去教堂。

*circle 圓圈

['sɝk!]

Everyone stands in a circle.
大家站成一個圓圈。

Draw a circle. 畫一個圓圈。

*city 城市

['sɪtɪ]

This city is too small. 這座城市太小了。

*class 上課；課程

[klæs]

When is the class over? 這堂課何時結束？

I like friends in my class. 我喜歡班上的朋友。

*classroom 教室

['klæs‚rum]

Let's clean the classroom. 我們來打掃教室吧。

*classmate 同班同學

['klæs‚met]

Suzzie and Teddy are classmates. 蘇西跟泰迪是同班同學。

*clean 清理，打掃；乾淨的 ● dirty

[klin]

Clean your teeth before going to bed.
就寢前要清潔牙齒。

CLOTHES
衣服

問孩子一年有哪些季節？夏天時穿什麼，冬天時穿什麼？上學時會穿什麼，睡覺時又會穿什麼？

給媽媽的

ribbon 髮帶

cap 帽子

blouse 女襯衫

backpack 背包

T-shirt T恤

skirt 裙子

shorts 寬鬆短運動褲

shoes 鞋子

bonnet 女帽

umbrella 雨傘

raincoat 雨衣

jumper 套頭毛衣

pants 褲子

rain boots 雨鞋

muffler 圍巾

sweater 毛衣

overcoat 大衣；外套

mitten 手套

nightgown 婦女或女孩的睡衣

dress shirt 西裝襯衫

necktie 領帶

belt 皮帶

slipper 拖鞋

doll's clothes 玩偶的衣服

dress 洋裝

socks 襪子

undershirt 內衣

underpants 內褲

✳climb 攀爬
[klaɪm]

A monkey is climbing up a tree.
一隻猴子爬到樹上去。

✳clock 鐘
[klɑk]

The clock is ticking.
這個鐘正在滴答滴答地走著。

✳close 關閉，閉上 ● open
[kloz]

Close your eyes. 閉上你的眼睛。

✳clothes 衣服
[kloz]

You have many clothes. 你有很多衣服。

✳cloud 雲
[klaud]

The mountain is covered with clouds.
這座山被雲籠罩著。

✴club 俱樂部；社團

[klʌb]

Which club do you want to join in?
你想加入哪個社團？

✴coat 外套，夾克

[kot]

A new coat is very warm. 新的外套非常溫暖。

✴coffee 咖啡

[ˈkɔfɪ]

Would you like a cup of coffee?
你想要來杯咖啡嗎？

✴coin 硬幣，錢幣

[kɔɪn]

Do you have any coins? 你身上有任何硬幣嗎？

✴cold 寒冷；冷的 ⊝ hot

[kold]

It is very cold outside today.
今天外面非常冷。

COLOR
顏色

black 黑色

gray 灰色

brown 棕色

blue 藍色

pink 粉紅色

yellow 黃色

white 白色

deep blue 深藍色

green 綠色

orange 橘色

red 紅色

purple 紫色

給媽媽的話

彩虹有七種顏色，紅橙黃綠藍靛紫。紅綠燈有三種顏色，紅綠黃。孩子能用英文說出各種顏色的名稱嗎？拿出一盒水彩及一張圖畫紙，請孩子挑出兩種顏色，各擠一些在調色盤上，再用畫筆調勻，讓孩子用英文說出新調的顏色。

✱color 顏色，色彩

[ˈkʌlɚ]

Which color do you like best? 你最喜歡哪種顏色？

comb 梳理

[kom]

Comb your hair. 梳你的頭髮。

✱come 來

[kʌm]

Come here, please. 請到這邊來。

Yes, I am coming. 是的，我來了。

✱computer 電腦

[kəmˈpjutɚ]

Where did you buy this computer? 你在哪裡買這台電腦？

✱cook 烹飪；廚師

[kʊk]

Do you love to cook? 你喜歡煮東西嗎？

cookie 餅乾

[ˈkuki]

May I have some cookies?
我可以吃些餅乾嗎？

COOKING
烹飪

stew 燉

steam 蒸

cut 切

stir 攪拌

mince 切碎

slice 切片

peel 削

給媽媽的話

廚房裡傳來陣陣的香味，什麼東西正在煮呢？模仿一種烹飪的動作，讓孩子猜猜這個動作是什麼，它的英文怎麼說。親手做一次麵包，請孩子也來幫忙攪麵粉、揉麵糰喔。

grill 火烤，碳烤

roast （烤箱）烘烤

bake 烘焙

mix 混合

boil 煮

deep fry 油炸

fry 煎

✳cool 微涼的，涼爽的

[kul]

It is very cool this morning. 今天早上非常涼爽。

✳copy 複製；抄寫

['kɑpɪ]

Can I copy your notes? 我可以抄你的筆記嗎？

corn 玉米

[kɔrn]

Feed corn to livestock.
餵家畜吃玉米。

✳corner 角落；轉角

['kɔrnɚ]

I am waiting for you at the corner.
我在轉角等你。

✳count 計算，數

[kaʊnt]

Count to ten. 從一數到十。

✳country 國家

['kʌntrɪ]

Which country are you from? 你來自哪個國家？

couple 配偶；一對

[ˈkʌpl̩]

They are a nice couple.
他們是很要好的一對。

*course 科目

[kors]

I take a course in English. 我修了一門英文課。

*cousin 堂（表）兄弟；堂（表）姊妹

[ˈkʌzn̩]

My cousin brought me here. 我堂弟帶我到這裡來。

*cover 覆蓋

[ˈkʌvɚ]

Snow covered the highway. 雪覆蓋了整條公路。

*cow 乳牛

[kaʊ]

We sold a brown cow yesterday.
我們昨天賣掉一頭棕色的乳牛。

✴crayon 蠟筆

[ˈkreən]

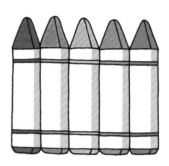

Crayons are children's best friends.
蠟筆是小朋友最佳的玩伴。

✴cream 奶油

[krim]

Suzzie likes ice cream . 蘇西喜歡冰淇淋。

crocodile 鱷魚

[ˈkrɑkəˌdaɪl]

I am not afraid of crocodiles.
我不怕鱷魚。

✴cross 橫越；交叉

[krɔs]

Cross your fingers. 把你的手指交叉（以祈求好運）。

Be careful when you cross the street. 當你過馬路時要小心。

✴cry 哭泣

[kraɪ]

The baby is crying. 這個寶寶正在哭。

✱cup 杯子

[kʌp]

Be careful not to break the cup.
小心不要打破杯子。

curtain 窗簾

[ˈkɝ·tn̩]

Would you draw
    down the curtain?
你能把窗簾拉起來嗎？

✱cut 切

[kʌt]

Let's cut an apple in half. 我們把蘋果切成兩半吧。

cute 可愛的

[kjut]

My brother is very cute. 我的弟弟非常可愛。

*dad / daddy 爸爸

[dæd / ˈdædɪ]

Daddy always comes home late.
爸爸總是很晚回家。

*dance 跳舞

[dæns]

Shall we dance? 我們跳支舞好嗎？

*danger 危險 ● safety

[ˈdendʒɚ]

There is no danger of flood in my town.
我的家鄉沒有淹水的危險。

✳dark 黑暗的 ⊖ light

[dɑrk]

dark green 墨綠色

Come home early before dark.
天黑前早點回家。

✳date 日期

[det]

What is the date today? 今天是幾月幾號？

Today is October 15. 今天是十月十五日。

✳daughter 女兒

[ˈdɔtɚ]

I have a daughter, Suzzie.
我有一個女兒蘇西。

✳day 日子；白天 ⊖ night

[de]

Have a nice day! 祝你有愉快的一天！

✳dead 死亡

[dɛd]

My dog was dead last year. 我的狗狗去年死掉了。

dear 親愛的

[dɪr]

Dear Suzzie 親愛的蘇西

*deep 深深的 ⬤ shallow

[dip]

How deep is this river?
這條河有多深呢？

*deer 鹿

[dɪr]

Have you ever seen a deer?
你看過鹿嗎？

dentist 牙醫

['dɛntɪst]

Alas! My father is a dentist.
哎呀！我的爸爸是牙醫。

department store 百貨公司

[dɪ'pɑrtmənt‚stor]

There are many department stores in my town.
我的家鄉有很多百貨公司。

*desk 桌子

[dɛsk]

I want to have my own desk.
我想要有我自己的桌子。

dessert 點心

[dɪˊzɝt]

I had cake for dessert. 我吃蛋糕當作點心。

*dial 打電話

[ˊdaɪəl]

Dial me at home. 到家打電話給我。

*diary 日記

[ˊdaɪərɪ]

You have to keep a diary every day.
你要每天寫日記。

*dictionary 字典

[ˊdɪkʃənˏɛrɪ]

He is a walking dictionary.
他是一部活字典。

✱die 去世 ⊜ live

[daɪ]

My grandfather died four years ago.
我的爺爺四年前去世了。

different 不一樣的 ⊜ same

[ˈdɪfərənt]

All children are different. 每個孩子都是不一樣的。

There are two different ways. 有兩種辦法。

difficult 困難的 ⊜ easy

[ˈdɪfəˌkəlt]

a difficult problem 一個困難的問題

The examination was very difficult this time.
這次的考試非常難。

✱dinner 正餐；晚餐

[ˈdɪnɚ]

What do you want to have for dinner?
你晚餐要吃什麼？

✱dirty 髒的 ⊜ clean

[ˈdɝtɪ]

a dirty face 一張髒臉

Your hands are very dirty.
你的手非常髒。

ice cream
冰淇淋

custard pudding
卡士達布丁

fresh juice
新鮮果汁

jam
果醬

scones
司康餅

cookie
餅乾

cherry pie
櫻桃派

DESSERT
點心

tea
茶

fruit jelly
水果果凍

cake
蛋糕

cocoa 可可

sandwich
三明治

parfait
冰甜點

＊dish 盤子

[dɪʃ]

I broke some dishes this morning.
我今天早上打破了一些盤子。

＊do 做

[du]

What are you doing? 你在做什麼？

I didn't do anything. 我沒有做任何事。

隨人稱代名詞而改變的 do 動詞變化

	主詞	現在式	過去式	過去分詞
第一人稱	單數 I 複數 we	do	did	done
第二人稱	單數 複數 you	do	did	done
第三人稱	單數 he/she/it	does	did	done
	複數 they	do	did	done

主詞是第三人稱單數且為現在式（過去式）時，do 動詞否定式要用 doesn't (didn't)。

＊doctor 醫生

[ˈdɑktɚ]

I want to be a doctor.
我想成為一位醫生。

✱dog 狗

[dɔg]

Is this your dog? 這是你的狗嗎？

What is your dog's name? 你的狗叫什麼名字？

✱doll 洋娃娃

[dɑl]

I don't like dolls.
我不喜歡洋娃娃。

✱dollar 一塊錢

[ˈdɑlɚ]

How much is it? 這個東西要多少錢？

It is sixty-five dollars. 它要六十五塊錢。

✱dolphin 海豚

[ˈdɑlfɪn]

Dolphins are very clever.
海豚非常聰明。

✱door 門

[dor]

How do you open this door?
你怎麼開這扇門？

Open the door, please. 請開門。

✸down 向下;在⋯下方 ● up
[daʊn]

Come down the hill. 走下山來。

Let's sit down. 我們坐下吧。

✸draw 畫畫
[drɔ]

I like drawing animals. 我喜歡畫動物。

✸dream 夢想;夢
[drim]

What is your dream? 你的夢想是什麼？

Good night and sweet dreams.
晚安，祝你有個好夢。

✸dress 禮服;洋裝
[drɛs]

an evening dress 一件晚禮服

Suzzie always puts on expensive dresses.
蘇西總是穿昂貴的洋裝。

✸drink 飲料
[drɪŋk]

What do you want to drink? 你想喝什麼飲料？

I want to drink some milk.
我想喝些牛奶。

*drive 開車
[draɪv]

> I can't drive yet. 我還不會開車。

*drop 水滴；滴落
[drɑp]

> a drop of rain 一滴雨
>
> Tears dropped from her eyes. 淚水從她眼裡滴下來。

*drum 鼓
[drʌm]

> a bass drum 大鼓　　a side drum 小鼓

*dry 乾的
[draɪ]

> a dry towel 一條乾毛巾
>
> Your clothes will soon dry. 你的衣服很快會乾。

*duck 鴨子
[dʌk]

> How many ducks are on the river?
> 河裡有幾隻鴨子？

Ee

E e [i]

each 每一個
[itʃ]

We each have our own rooms.
我們每一個人都有自己的房間。

Let's get along with each other.
讓我們彼此陪伴吧。

each other 是「彼此」的意思。

＊ear 耳朵
[ɪr]

A rabbit has a pair of long ears.
兔子有一對長長的耳朵。

＊early 早；及早 ○ late
[ˈɝlɪ]

I got up early this morning. 我今天早上很早起床。

✱ earth 地球

[ɝθ]

The earth moves round the sun. 地球繞著太陽轉。

✱ east 東邊

[ist]

The sun rises in the east.
太陽從東邊升起。

✱ easy 容易的 ● difficult

[ˈizɪ]

Try it, it is easy. 試試看，那很容易。

✱ eat 吃

[it]

What did you eat for lunch? 你午餐吃了什麼？

Don't eat snow! 不要吃雪！

✱ egg 蛋

[ɛg]

fried eggs 煎蛋

The egg is rotten. 這顆蛋臭掉了。

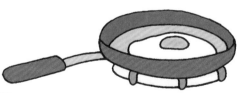

eight 八

[et]

I am eight years old. 我八歲。

either 也不；兩者任何一個

['iðɚ]

Teddy doesn't like vegetables, either. 泰迪也不喜歡蔬菜。

I don't know either boy. 那兩個男孩任何一個我都不認識。

elbow 手肘

['ɛlbo]

Suzzie is sitting with her elbows on the table.
蘇西把手肘靠在桌上坐著。

elephant 大象

['ɛləfənt]

How do you put an elephant
into a refrigerator?
你要怎麼把一隻大象放進冰箱呢？

elevator 電梯

['ɛlə,vetɚ]

There is an elevator in my apartment.
我的公寓裡有一座電梯。

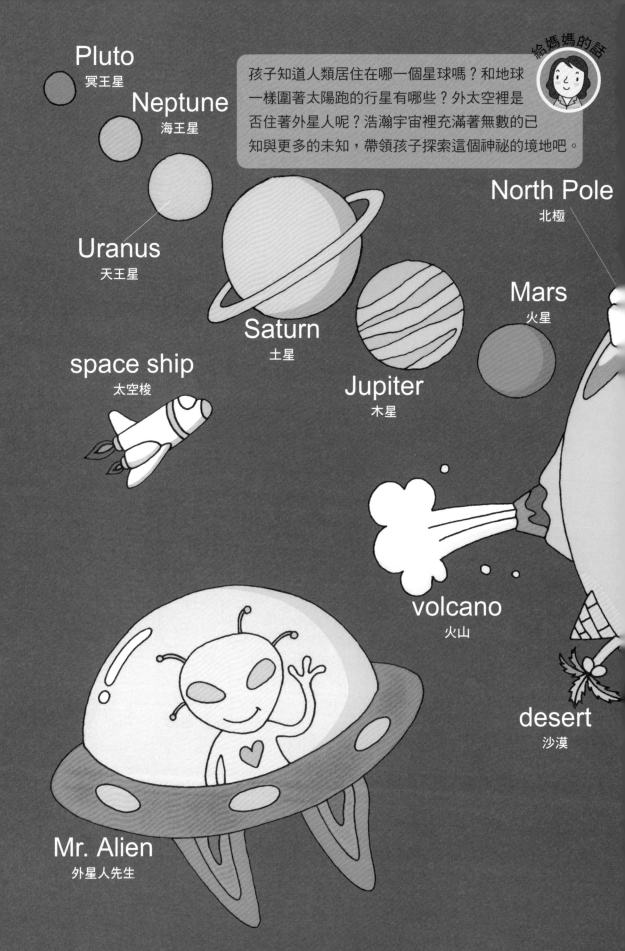

Pluto
冥王星

Neptune
海王星

Uranus
天王星

North Pole
北極

Saturn
土星

Mars
火星

space ship
太空梭

Jupiter
木星

volcano
火山

desert
沙漠

Mr. Alien
外星人先生

孩子知道人類居住在哪一個星球嗎？和地球一樣圍著太陽跑的行星有哪些？外太空裡是否住著外星人呢？浩瀚宇宙裡充滿著無數的已知與更多的未知，帶領孩子探索這個神祕的境地吧。

給媽媽的話

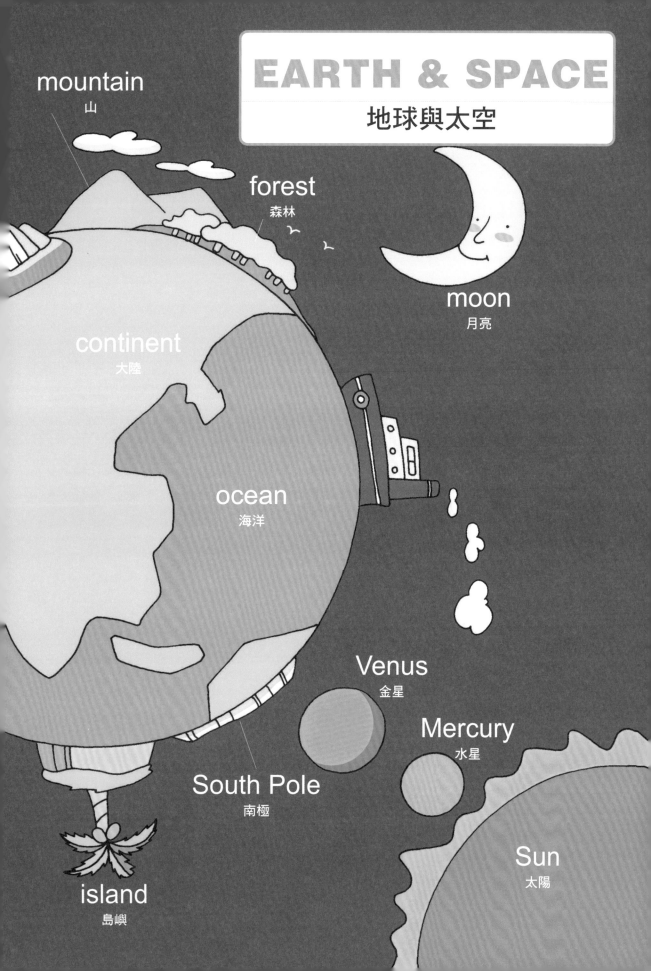

EARTH & SPACE
地球與太空

mountain
山

forest
森林

moon
月亮

continent
大陸

ocean
海洋

Venus
金星

Mercury
水星

South Pole
南極

island
島嶼

Sun
太陽

eleven 十一

[ɪˈlɛvn̩]

I slept for eleven hours yesterday. 我昨天睡了十一個小時。

✻empty 空的 ⇔ full

[ˈɛmptɪ]

an empty house 一個空蕩蕩的房子

Why is my basket empty? 為什麼我的籃子是空的？

✻end 結尾

[ɛnd]

the end of the day 一天的結尾

There is no end to your story.
你的故事沒有結尾。

✻engine 引擎

[ˈɛndʒən]

Start the engine now! 現在啟動引擎！

✻enjoy 享受；喜歡

[ɪnˈdʒɔɪ]

I enjoyed my time.
我享受我的時間。

Most people enjoy sweets.
大部分的人喜歡甜點。

∗enough 足夠的
[ə'nʌf]

It isn't good enough. 那樣不夠好。

Take it easy. You have enough time.
放輕鬆。你有足夠的時間。

∗eraser 橡皮擦
[ɪ'resɚ]

Why do you collect erasers?
為什麼你要蒐集橡皮擦？

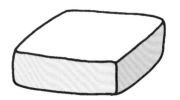

Europe 歐洲
['jurəp]

Someday I will visit Europe.
有天我要拜訪歐洲。

∗evening 晚上
['ivnɪŋ]

Every evening, we take a walk together.
每天晚上，我們一起散步。

∗every 每一個
['ɛvrɪ]

Every boy likes me. 每一個男孩都喜歡我。

Forget every word she said. 忘記她說過的每一句話吧。

*example 例子

[ɪgˊzæmp!]

Here is an example. 這裡有一個例子。

*excellent 優秀的，很好的

[ˊɛks!ənt]

I have an excellent memory.
我有很好的記憶。

*excite 讓人振奮

[ɪkˊsaɪt]

His song excited me.
他的歌讓我很振奮。

*excuse 原諒；藉口

[ɪkˊskjuz]

Excuse me. 對不起。

Don't give me any excuses. 不要給我任何藉口。

*exercise 運動；練習

[ˊɛksɚˌsaɪz]

Exercise can give you energy.
運動可以給你活力。

spelling exercises 拼音練習

∗expensive 昂貴的 ↔ cheap

[ɪkˈspɛnsɪv]

The car is very expensive. 這輛車非常昂貴。

∗eye 眼睛

[aɪ]

Close your eyes. 閉上你的眼睛。

eyebrow 眉毛

[ˈaɪˌbraʊ]

He raised his eyebrows.
他揚起了他的眉毛。

首先，找一張舒適的沙發或椅子，靠在床頭也可以。
放鬆心情，讓孩子依偎在懷裡。帶著孩子一起唸生字，
生字旁如果有插圖，唸完生字後，
請用生動活潑的語調講解插圖，增進孩子連結圖像與聲音的記憶能力。

[ɛf]

*face 臉

[fes]

a sad face 一張憂傷的臉

He has a funny face.
他有一張滑稽的臉。

*fact 事實

[fækt]

It is a fact that I wasn't late! 我沒有遲到是事實！

fail 失敗

[fel]

If you fail, then try it again!
如果你失敗了，就再試一次！

FACE
臉

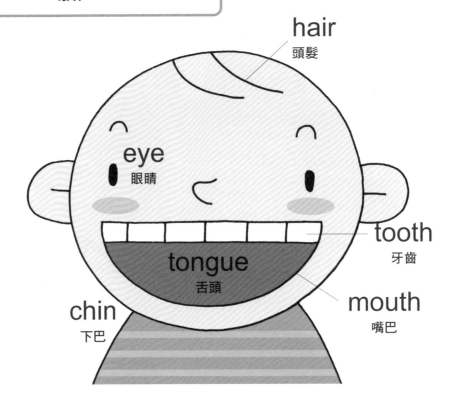

hair
頭髮

eye
眼睛

tooth
牙齒

tongue
舌頭

mouth
嘴巴

chin
下巴

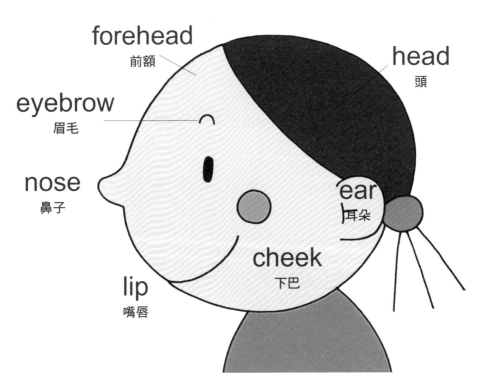

forehead
前額

head
頭

eyebrow
眉毛

nose
鼻子

ear
耳朵

lip
嘴唇

cheek
下巴

the index finger
the forefinger
食指

the middle finger
the long finger
中指

the thumb
the big finger
大姆指

the ring finger
無名指

the little finger
小指

✴**fair** 美好的；公平的

[fɛr]

a fair play　一場不錯的演出

It isn't fair! 那不公平！

fairy 仙女似的

[ˈfɛrɪ]

a fairy tale　一則童話故事

✴**fall** 落下；秋天 ⊖ autumn

[fɔl]

The snow is falling fast.
雪下得很快。

Why do leaves change their color in fall?
為什麼葉子會在秋天改變顏色？

---

famous 有名的

[ˈfeməs]

a famous writer 一位有名的作家

I want to be a famous photographer.
我想成為一位有名的攝影師。

✴**family** 家人

[ˈfæməlɪ]

My family are all well. 我的家人都很好。

FAMILY
家族

grandfather
祖父

grandmother
祖母

uncle
伯伯

aunt
伯母

father
爸爸

mother
媽媽

cousin
堂姐

brother-in-law
姐夫

sister
姐姐

I 我

brother
弟弟

nephew
姪子

niece
姪女

給媽媽的話

「我的家庭真可愛／整潔美滿又安康／姊妹兄弟很和氣／父母都慈祥／…」孩子知道自己的家族裡有哪些人嗎？用英文如何稱呼他們呢？和中文相比，英文裡親戚的稱呼簡單多了唷。

A
B
C
D
E
F
G
H
I
J
K
L
M
N
O
P
Q
R
S
T
U
V
W
X
Y
Z

＊**far** 遠的 ● near

[fɑr]

My house is not far from here.
我的家離這裡不遠。

＊**farm** 畜牧場；農地

[fɑrm]

a fish farm 一座漁池

＊**fast** 急快的 ● slow

[fæst]

a fast train 一列高速火車

Suzzie runs really fast.
蘇西跑得真快。

＊**fat** 肥胖的 ● thin

[fæt]

Many Americans are too fat. 很多美國人都太胖了。

fate 命運

[fet]

His fate was to be a hero. 他註定要成為一位英雄。

*father 爸爸
[ˈfɑðɚ]

My father is really handsome. 我爸爸真帥。

*feel 感覺
[fil]

I feel hungry.
我覺得餓了。

The air feels cold.
空氣感覺起來很冷。

*few 少量的，幾個
[fju]

Teddy has few friends. 泰迪只有幾個朋友。

*field 田野
[fild]

My parents work in the fields all day.
我的父母整天在田裡工作。

*fight 打架
[faɪt]

Two boys are fighting on the street.
兩個男孩正在街上打架。

farm tractor 農用拖拉機

stream 小河

cow 母牛

horse 馬

field 田地

barn 穀倉

mole 鼴鼠

pig 豬

rooster 公雞

sheep 綿羊

hen 母雞

chicken coop 雞籠

egg 蛋

chicks 小雞

孩子去過養著各種動物、種植各種蔬菜的農場，還是只在網路上玩開心農場呢？農場常見的那些動物，牠們的叫聲如何啊？試著模仿農場動物的叫聲，讓孩子猜猜看那是什麼動物。

FARM
農場

fence
籬笆

farmhouse
農舍

goat
山羊

cat
貓

frog
青蛙

duck
鴨子

dog
狗

mouse
老鼠

pond
池塘

*fill 裝滿

[fɪl]

Fill the bottle with water. 把瓶子裝滿水。

*film 影片

[fɪlm]

a roll of film 一捲底片　a film actor 一位電影演員

*find 找到

[faɪnd]

You can find strawberries in the woods.
你可以在樹林裡找到草莓。

*fine 好的

[faɪn]

It is fine today. 今天天氣很好。

*finger 手指

[ˈfɪŋgɚ]

A hand has five fingers.
一隻手有五根手指。

*finish 完成

[ˊfɪnɪʃ]

Have you finished your dinner? 你吃完晚餐了嗎？

*fire 火

[faɪr]

A fire broke out last night. 昨晚有一場火災。

*fish 魚

[fɪʃ]

So many fishes are swimming in the pond.

很多魚在池塘裡游泳。

five 五

[faɪv]

They have five children. 他們有五個小孩。

*fix 修理

[fɪks]

How did you fix it? 你怎麼修理它？

*flag 旗子

[flæg]

a Korean national flag 一支韓國國旗

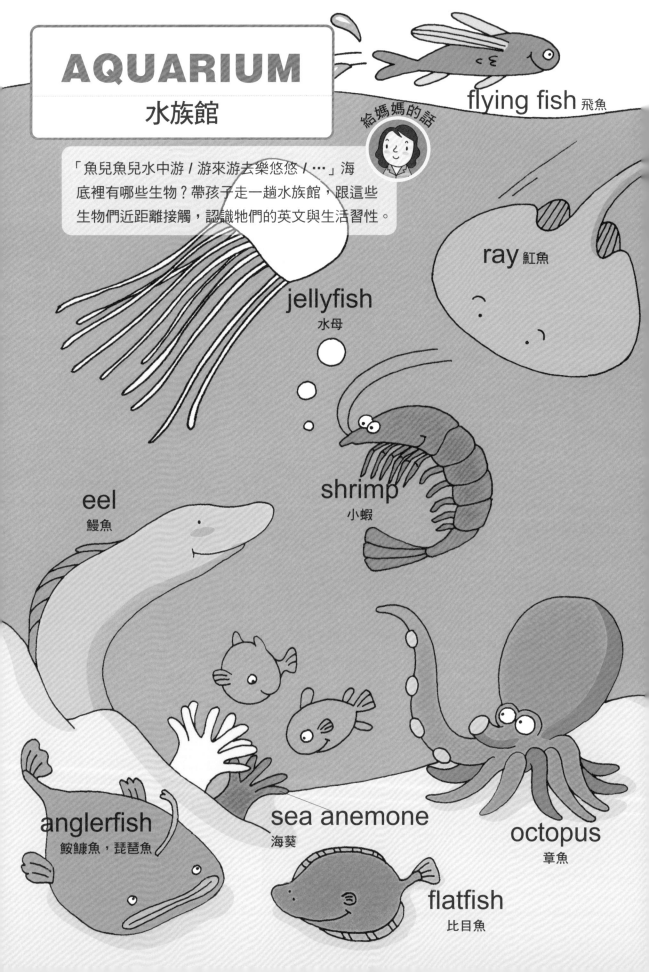

AQUARIUM
水族館

給媽媽的話

「魚兒魚兒水中游／游來游去樂悠悠／…」海底裡有哪些生物？帶孩子走一趟水族館，跟這些生物們近距離接觸，認識牠們的英文與生活習性。

flying fish 飛魚

ray 魟魚

jellyfish
水母

shrimp
小蝦

eel
鰻魚

anglerfish
鮟鱇魚，琵琶魚

sea anemone
海葵

octopus
章魚

flatfish
比目魚

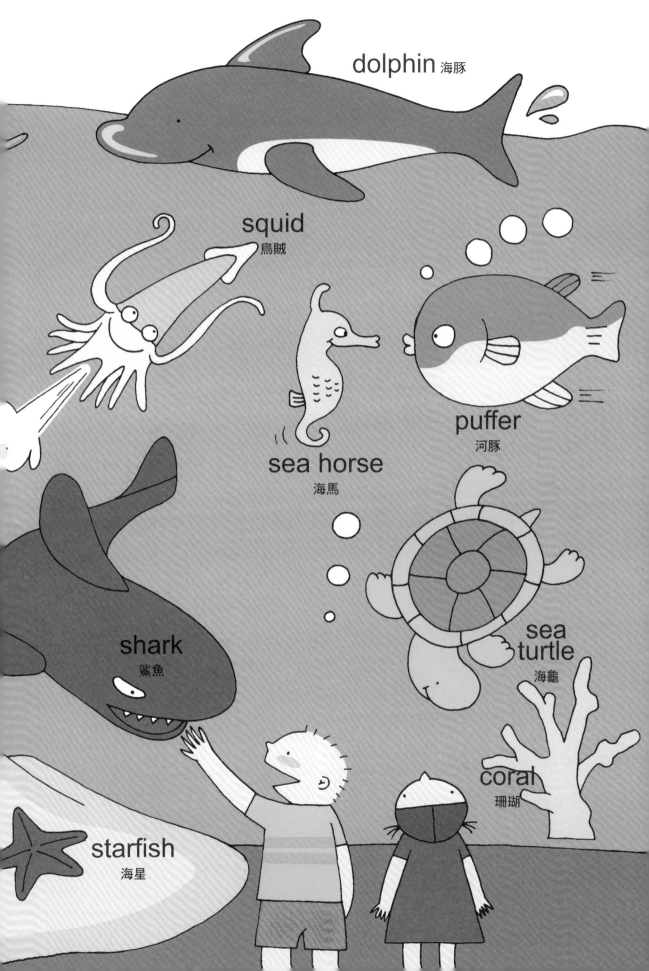

A
B
C
D
E
F
G
H
I
J
K
L
M
N
O
P
Q
R
S
T
U
V
W
X
Y
Z

flat 平坦的

[flæt]

Teddy was lying flat on the ground.
泰迪平躺在地上。

The land under the sea is not flat. 海底下的陸地並不平坦。

✲floor 地板；樓層

[flor]

I feel the floor shaking. 我感到地板在搖。

Which floor are you on? 你住在幾樓？

✲flower 花

['flauɚ]

Which flower do you like best?
你最喜歡哪一種花？

✲fly 飛翔

[flaɪ]

I want to fly like a bird.
我想像小鳥一樣飛翔。

✲follow 跟隨

['fɑlo]

Why do you follow me? 為什麼你要跟著我？

*food 食物
[fud]

Can I bring food to camp? 我能帶食物到營地去嗎？

The food is really delicious. 這種食物真好吃。

*fool 傻瓜
[ful]

I must be a fool. 我一定是個傻瓜。

*foot 腳
[fʊt]

I have the biggest foot in the class.
在班上我的腳是最大的。

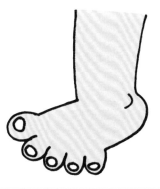

*for 給；維持
[fɔr]

This is a present for you. 這是給你的禮物。

My brother cried for two hours.
我的弟弟哭了兩個小時。

*forget 忘記
[fɚˈgɛt]

Don't forget my birthday. 別忘了我的生日。

FLOWER
花

美麗的花朵有美麗的稱呼，中英文都是。孩子知道這些花的名字嗎？

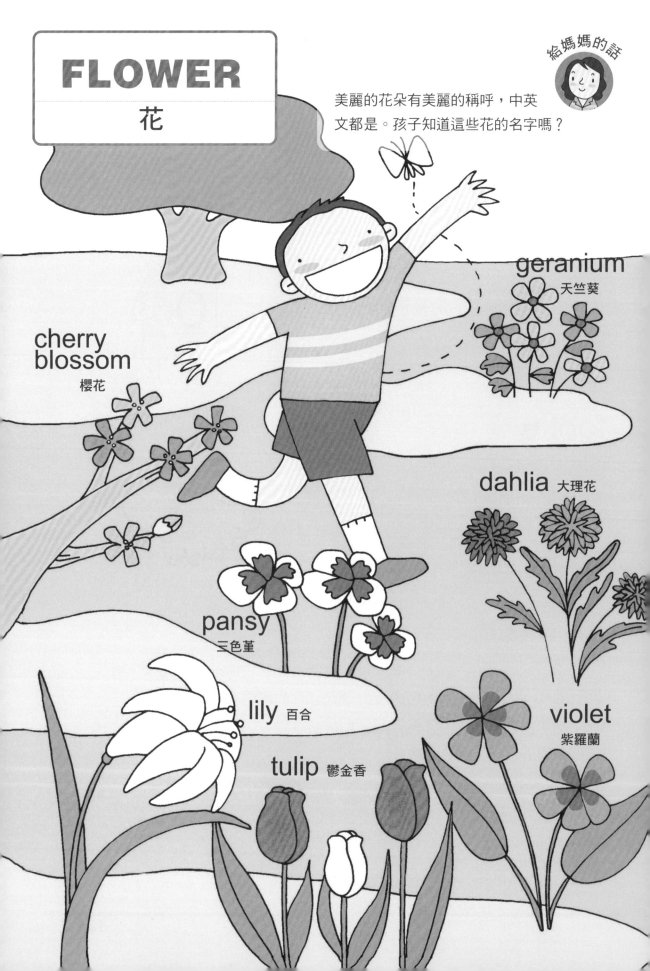

geranium 天竺葵

cherry blossom 櫻花

dahlia 大理花

pansy 三色菫

lily 百合

violet 紫羅蘭

tulip 鬱金香

rose 玫瑰

cosmos 大波斯菊

sunflower 向日葵

daisy 雛菊

poppy 罌粟花

dandelion 蒲公英

clover 三葉草

carnation 康乃馨

chrysanthemum 菊花

*fork 叉子

[fɔrk]

It is easier to use forks than chopsticks.
用叉子比用筷子容易。

four 四

[fɔr]

I slept only four hours last night.
我昨天晚上只睡了四小時。

fox 狐狸

[fɑks]

A fox is a cunning animal.
狐狸是狡猾的動物。

*free 自由的

[fri]

Let the bird free. 讓小鳥自由吧。

I am free on Saturday night. 我星期六晚上有空。

*fresh 新鮮的

[frɛʃ]

These cggs are fresh. 這些蛋很新鮮。

Friday 星期五

[ˈfraɪˌde]

How about meeting next Friday?
下星期五見面好嗎?

∗friend 朋友

[frɛnd]

We are the best friends.
我們是最好的朋友。

frog 青蛙

[frɑg]

Frogs eat flies.
青蛙吃蒼蠅。

∗from 從,離

[frɑm]

The school is far from here. 學校離這裡很遠。

∗front 在前;在⋯前面

[frʌnt]

There is an apple tree in front of my house.
有一棵蘋果樹在我家的前面。

*fruit 水果
[frut]

Fresh fruits are good for health.
新鮮水果有益身體健康。

*full 裝滿的 ○ empty
[fʊl]

Do not talk with your mouth full.
嘴巴含著東西時別說話。

*fun 有趣的，好玩的
[fʌn]

It was fun picking shells on the beach.
在海邊撿貝殼很好玩。

funny 有趣的 ○ interesting
['fʌnɪ]

My teacher is funny.
我的老師很有趣。

future 未來
['fjutʃɚ]

The future is yours! 未來是屬於你的！

FRUIT
水果

pineapple 鳳梨

orange 橘子

banana 香蕉

plum 李子

lemon 檸檬

watermelon 西瓜

melon 香瓜

strawberry 草莓

peach 桃子

save 50%

apple 蘋果

pear 梨子

cherry 櫻桃

grape 葡萄

給媽媽的話

首先，找一張舒適的沙發或椅子，靠在床頭也可以。
放鬆心情，讓孩子依偎在懷裡。帶著孩子一起唸生字，
生字旁如果有插圖，唸完生字後，
請用生動活潑的語調講解插圖，增進孩子連結圖像與聲音的記憶能力。

G g [dʒi]

＊game 遊戲

[gem]

Do you like games? 你喜歡遊戲嗎？

garbage 垃圾

[ˈgɑrbɪdʒ]

I don't like to throw away garbage.
我不喜歡丟垃圾。

＊garden 花園

[ˈgɑrdn̩]

a secret garden 一座祕密花園

Let's have a tea break in the garden.
我們在花園裡來個下午茶吧。

✳gas 瓦斯
[gæs]

Turn off the gas. 把瓦斯關掉。

✳gate 門,出入口
[get]

I can't find the gate without my glasses.
我沒有眼鏡無法找到門。

gather 聚集
[ˈgæðɚ]

We gathered around the campfire.
我們聚集在營火周圍。

Suzzie gathered roses in the garden.
蘇西在花園裡採集玫瑰花。

✳gentle 溫和的
[ˈʤɛntl̩]

He is gentle with children.
他對孩子很溫和。

✳Germany 德國
[ˈʤɝ·mənɪ]

My sister studies in Germany.
我的姐姐在德國讀書。

★get 拿到，取得；抵達
[gɛt]

Did you get some money? 你拿到了一些錢嗎？

How do we get there? 我們怎麼到那裡？

giant 巨人
[ˈdʒaɪənt]

Last night, I met a giant in my dream.
昨天晚上，我在夢裡遇到了一個巨人。

gift 禮物
[gɪft]

We exchanged gifts with each other.
我們互相交換禮物。

giraffe 長頸鹿
[dʒəˈræf]

A giraffe has a long neck.
長頸鹿有長長的脖子。

★girl 女孩
[gɝl]

You are a good girl.
妳是個好女孩。

★give 給予
[gɪv]

Why don't you give me a birthday present?
你何不送我一份生日禮物？

Give me one more chance. 再給我一次機會。

★glad 高興的
[glæd]

I am very glad to meet you. 我很高興見到你。

I am glad to hear that. 我很高興聽到那件事。

★glass 玻璃杯
[glæs]

My sister always breaks a glass.
我妹妹總是打破玻璃杯。

glasses 眼鏡
[ˈglæsɪz]

I can't see anything without my glasses.
我沒有眼鏡看不到任何東西。

★glove 手套
[glʌv]

We put on gloves in winter.
冬天時我們戴上手套。

✳go 去
[go]

We go to school every day. 我們每天去上學。

現在式　　過去式　　過去分詞

go　-　went　-　gone

但是，句子的主詞若是第三人稱現在式時態，像 he / she / it ，
則動詞 go 就要改成 goes。

She goes to church on Sunday.

她星期天會去做禮拜。

Suzzie went home at five. 蘇西五點回家。

goat 山羊
[got]

Goats like eating weeds.
山羊喜歡吃雜草。

✳God 上帝
[gɑd]

God bless you. 上帝祝福你。

✳gold 金子
[gold]

All that glitters is not gold.
那些閃爍的未必都是金子。
（單憑外表不可靠。）

golf 高爾夫
[gɑlf]

Golf is a kind of sports.
高爾夫是一種運動。

G

★good 好的 ⊝ bad
[gʊd]

Read a good book. 讀一本好書。

goose 鵝 geese
[gus]

Geese can't fly. 鵝不會飛。

 goose 的複數是 geese [gis]。

gorilla 大猩猩
[gəˊrɪlə]

You look like a gorilla.
你看起來像個大猩猩。

grade 分數；年級
[gred]

What grade are you in? 你讀幾年級？

grammar 文法
[´græmɚ]

English grammar is not difficult. 英文文法並不難。

＊grandfather / grandpa 爺爺
[´grænd‚faðɚ / ´grændpɑ]

My grandfather is good at singing.
我爺爺很會唱歌。

＊grandmother / grandma 奶奶
[´grænd‚mɑðɚ / ´grændmɑ]

My grandmother is ninety years old this year.
我奶奶今年九十歲。

＊grape 葡萄
[grep]

We found grapes in the woods.
我們在樹林裡找到葡萄。

＊grass 草
[græs]

Keep off the grass. 勿踐踏草地。

grasshopper 蚱蜢

['græsˌhɑpɚ]

Grasshoppers are hopping around the grass.
蚱蜢在草叢附近跳來跳去。

G

*gray 灰色；灰色的

[gre]

Skies are gray. 天空是灰色的。

*great 偉大的

[gret]

You are great! 你好棒！

It was great fun. 它超有趣。

*green 綠色；綠色的

[grin]

Your eyes are green. 你的眼睛是綠色的。

*ground 地面

[graund]

A mole lives under the ground.
鼴鼠住在地下。

---

*group 群，團體

[grup]

Ants live in groups. 螞蟻成群住在一起。

*grow 長大

[gro]

A baby is growing day by day.
寶寶一天天長大。

guest 客人

[gɛst]

How many guests are here? 這裡有多少客人？

guide 引導

[gaɪd]

The stars guide us in the sea.
在海上星星引導我們。

*guitar 吉他

[gɪˈtɑr]

My uncle gave me a guitar as a birthday present.
我叔叔送我一把吉他當作生日禮物。

gun 槍

[gʌn]

I have never seen a gun closely.
我從來沒有近距離看過槍。

H h [etʃ]

＊hair 頭髮

[hɛɚ]

Suzzie has black hair.
蘇西有一頭黑髮。

＊half 一半，二分之一

[hæf]

The half of six is three.
六的二分之一是三。

Let's divide the banana in half.
我們把香蕉切成兩半。

＊hall 會堂

[hɔl]

a city hall 一座市政廳

＊hamburger 漢堡

['hæmbɚgɚ]

How many hamburgers can you eat?
你可以吃幾個漢堡？

＊hand 手

[hænd]

Wash your hands quickly. 快點把手洗乾淨。

Look at your left hand. 看你的左手。

＊handle 把手

['hændl̩]

Would you wipe the handle?
你可以擦一擦這個把手嗎？

hang 掛上

[hæŋ]

Hang your coat on the hook.
把你的西裝掛在掛勾上。

＊happen 發生

['hæpən]

Tell me what happened.
告訴我發生什麼事了。

✱happy 快樂的 ⊖ unhappy, sad
[ˈhæpɪ]

I am happy. 我很快樂。

Happy birthday to you!
祝你生日快樂！

✱hard 堅硬的；困難的
[hɑrd]

This bread is very hard.
這個麵包很硬。

The problem is not so hard, isn't it?
這個問題並不那麼難，不是嗎？

✱hat 帽子
[hæt]

Why are you wearing hat on a rainy day?
為什麼你在下雨天戴著帽子？

✱hate 討厭
[het]

I really hate snakes.
我真的討厭蛇。

I hate you. 我討厭你。

*have 擁有

[hæv]

Do you have a violin? 你有小提琴嗎？

隨人稱代名詞而改變的 have 動詞變化		
	單數	複數
第一人稱	I have	we have
第二人稱	you have	you have
第三人稱	he, she, it has	they have

*he 他

[hi]

He is a liar. 他是一個騙子。

*head 頭

[hɛd]

A fly is on your head.
一隻蒼蠅在你的頭上。

health 健康

[hɛlθ]

Suzzie is in good health.
蘇西很健康。

*hear 聽見

[hɪr]

Can you hear me? 你聽得到我嗎？

*heart 心；心臟

[hɑrt]

My grandfather has a weak heart.
我爺爺的心臟很脆弱。

You are always in my heart.
你總是在我的心裡。

*heavy 重的 ⊖ light

[ˈhɛvɪ]

This bag is too heavy for me. 這個袋子對我來說太重了。

helicopter 直升機

[ˈhɛlɪkɑptɚ]

Helicopters are noisy.
直升機很吵。

*hello 哈囉

[həˈlo]

Hello, it is nice to meet you. 哈囉，很高興認識你。

Hello, this is Suzzie. 哈囉，我是蘇西。

*help 幫忙

[hɛlp]

Can you help me?
你能幫我嗎？

✱hen 母雞 ⬌ cock, rooster

[hɛn]

A hen lays many eggs. 一隻母雞孵很多蛋。

her 她的；她

[hɝ]

This is her computer. 這是她的電腦。

I like her. 我喜歡她。

✱here 這裡

[hɪr]

I will stay here till tomorrow.
我會在這裡住到明天。

✱hi 嗨

[haɪ]

Hi, Suzzie.
嗨，蘇西。

✱hide 躲藏

[haɪd]

Why are you hiding? 為什麼你要躲起來？

✱high 高的

[haɪ]

How high can you jump? 你可以跳多高？

⋆hiking 遠足，健行
[haɪkɪŋ]

We are going to go hiking.
我們即將要去遠足。

⋆hill 山丘，丘陵
[hɪl]

There is a yellow house on the hill.
山丘上有一棟黃色的房子。

history 歷史
[ˈhɪstərɪ]

Do you know well about Japanese history?
你很了解日本歷史嗎？

⋆hit 打擊；撞到
[hɪt]

Teddy hit me on the head.
泰迪打我的頭。

Hit the target! 正中目標！

hobby 嗜好
[ˈhɑbɪ]

What is your hobby? 你的嗜好是什麼？

*hold 捉住

[hold]

Hold my hand.
握住我的手。

*hole 洞

[hol]

A dog is digging a hole.
一隻狗正在挖洞。

*holiday 假日

[ˈhɑləˌde]

I hope to take a holiday for a week.
我希望可以放一個禮拜的假。

*home 家

[hom]

Suzzie has not come home yet.
蘇西還沒有回家。

homework 家庭作業

[ˈhomˌwɝk]

Did you finish your homework? 你做完功課了嗎？

Can you help me with my homework?

你能幫我寫作業嗎？

*hope 希望

[hop]

I hope to be a grown-up.
我希望當個大人。

*horse 馬

[hɔrs]

I love riding a horse.
我喜歡騎馬。

horror 恐怖

[ˈhɔrɚ]

a horror film 一部恐怖電影

*hose 水管

[hoz]

My mother is watering her garden with a water hose.
我媽媽正在用水管幫她的花園澆水。

*hospital 醫院

[ˈhɑspɪtl̩]

The beggar died at the hospital. 這個乞丐在醫院去世了。

*hot 熱的

[hɑt]

Today is really hot. 今天真的很熱。

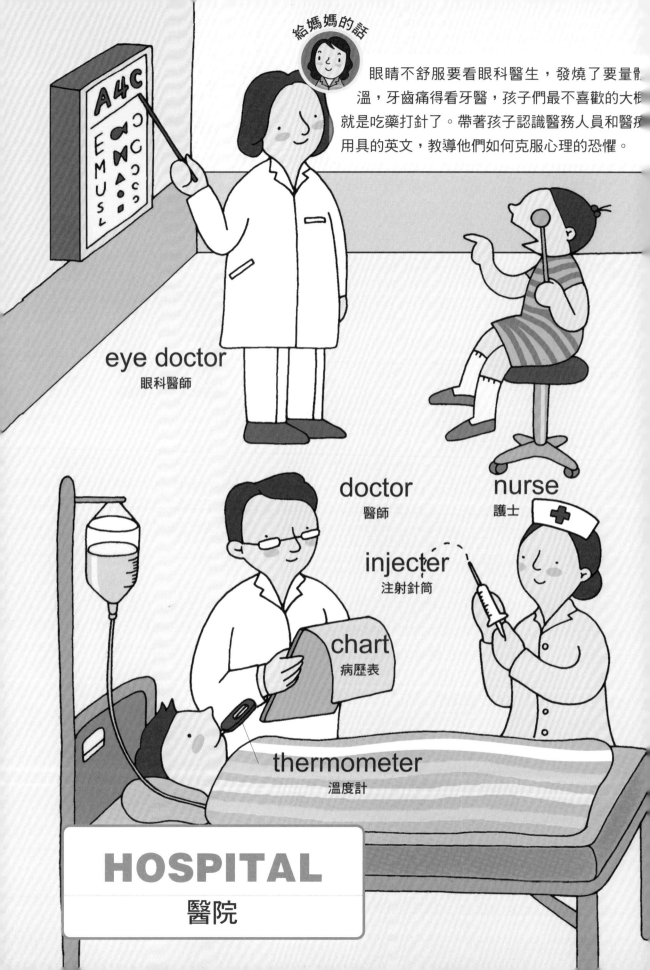

eye doctor
眼科醫師

doctor
醫師

nurse
護士

injecter
注射針筒

chart
病歷表

thermometer
溫度計

HOSPITAL
醫院

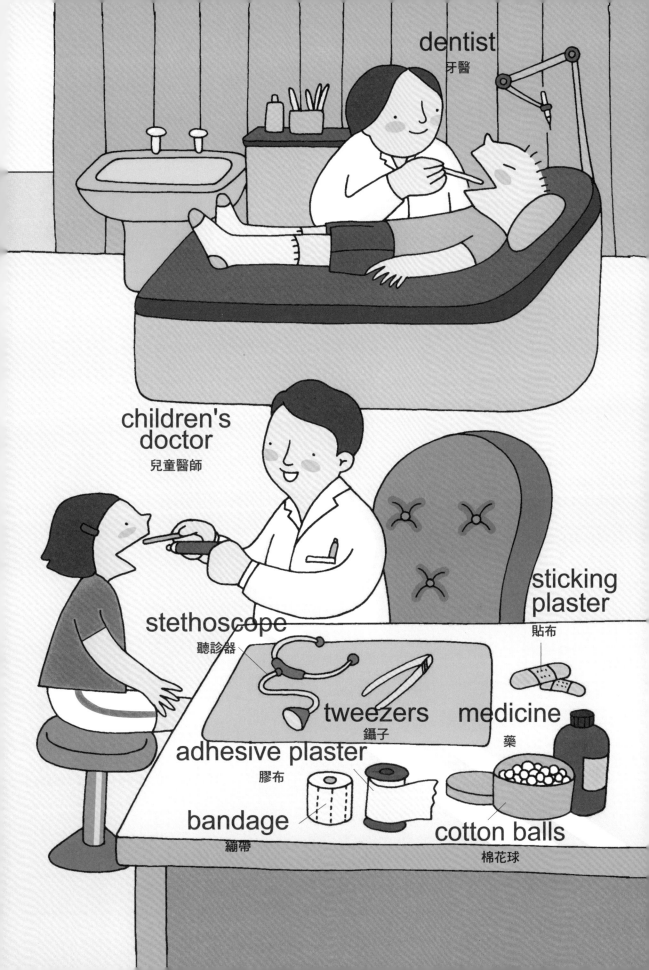

dentist
牙醫

children's
doctor
兒童醫師

sticking
plaster
貼布

stethoscope
聽診器

tweezers
鑷子

medicine
藥

adhesive plaster
膠布

bandage
繃帶

cotton balls
棉花球

*hotel 旅館

[ho'tɛl]

This hotel is dirty. 這間旅館很髒。

We stayed at the hotel for two nights.
我們在旅館住了兩夜。

*hour 小時

[aʊr]

Suzzie plays the violin for two hours every day.
蘇西每天拉小提琴兩個小時。

*house 房子

[haʊs]

Who is in the house?
誰在房子裡面？

*how 如何；真是

[haʊ]

How did you make it? 你是如何做到的？

How beautiful you are! 你好美麗呀！

*hundred 一百

['hʌndrəd]

hundreds of people 數以百計的人們

✱hungry 飢餓的

[ˈhʌŋgrɪ]

I am hungry. 我餓了。

I am so hungry. 我好餓。

hunt 打獵

[hʌnt]

We shouldn't hunt endangered animals
我們不應該獵捕瀕臨絕種的動物。

✱hurry 趕快

[ˈhɝɪ]

Hurry up! 快一點！　Don't hurry. 別急。

✱hurt 傷害；疼痛

[hɝt]

Your words hurt my feelings.
你的話傷了我的心。

My arm still hurts. 我的手臂還在痛。

husband 丈夫 ↔ wife

[ˈhʌzbənd]

My husband loves to cook.
我的丈夫喜歡煮菜。

Ii

給媽媽的話

首先，找一張舒適的沙發或椅子，靠在床頭也可以。
放鬆心情，讓孩子依偎在懷裡。帶著孩子一起唸生字，
生字旁如果有插圖，唸完生字後，
請用生動活潑的語調講解插圖，增進孩子連結圖像與聲音的記憶能力。

[aɪ]

*I 我
[aɪ]

I am Suzzie. 我是蘇西。

*ice 冰塊
[aɪs]

Fill the glass with ice, please.
請把杯子裝滿冰塊。

ice cream 冰淇淋
[ˌaɪsˈkrim]

Teddy likes ice cream. 泰迪喜歡冰淇淋。

Hurry up, the ice cream is melting. 快點，冰淇淋要溶化了。

*idea 點子
[aɪ'diə]

Do you have any ideas?
你有任何點子嗎？

That is a good idea!
好點子！

*if 假如
[ɪf]

If I were a bird, I could fly to Suzzie.
假如我是一隻鳥，我就能飛到蘇西身邊。

*ill 生病的
[ɪl]

Babies become ill easily. 寶寶很容易生病。

important 重要的
[ɪm'pɔrtṇt]

Why is love important?
為什麼愛很重要？

*in 在…裡面
[ɪn]

There is a cat in the box.
盒子裡有一隻貓。

∗ink 墨水

[ɪŋk]

Don't write a name with red ink.
別用紅墨水寫名字。

insect 昆蟲

[ˈɪnsɛkt]

Fabre studied many kinds of insects.
法布爾研究了各式各樣的昆蟲。

inside 在…裡面 ● outside

[ˈɪnˈsaɪd]

There is someone
    inside the house.
有人在房子裡。

∗interesting 有趣的

[ˈɪntərɪstɪŋ]

It was a really interesting movie.
那真是一部有趣的電影。

Internet 網路

[ˈɪntɚˌnɛt]

The Internet provides a lot of information.
網路提供很多資訊。

INSECT
昆蟲

給媽媽的話

自然界裡有許多比人體微小好多好多的小動物們，牠們是昆蟲。孩子能用英文說出幾種昆蟲呢？這些昆蟲他們都親眼見過嗎？

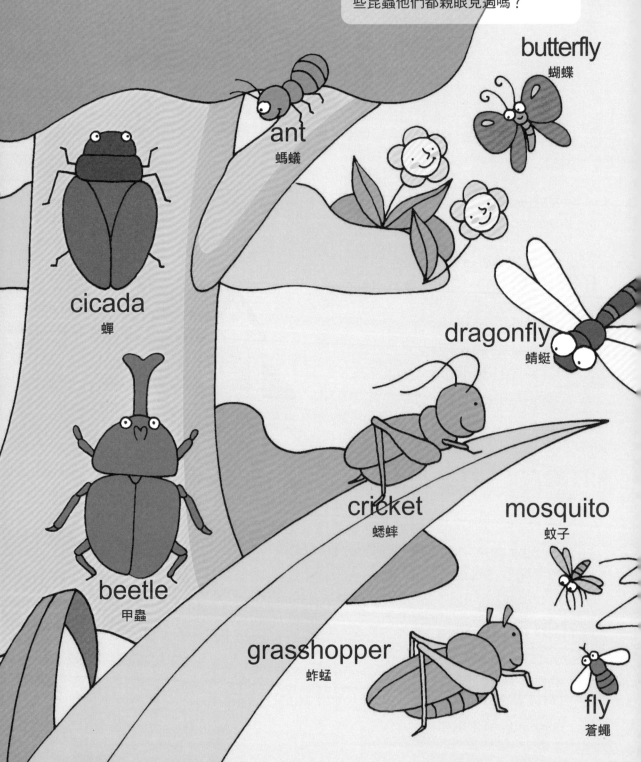

butterfly
蝴蝶

ant
螞蟻

cicada
蟬

dragonfly
蜻蜓

beetle
甲蟲

cricket
蟋蟀

mosquito
蚊子

grasshopper
蚱蜢

fly
蒼蠅

firefly 螢火蟲

moth 蛾

katydid 螽斯

bee 蜜蜂

stag beetle 鍬形蟲

mantis 螳螂

caterpillar 毛毛蟲

ladybug 瓢蟲

cockroach 蟑螂

*into 到…裡面

['ɪntu]

A pig came into my room.
一隻豬來到我的房間裡。

*introduce 介紹

[ˌɪntrəˈdjus]

Let me introduce my sister to you.
讓我介紹我的妹妹給你認識。

is 是

[ɪz]

My name is Suzzie.
我的名字是蘇西。

There is a pretty butterfly.
有一隻漂亮的蝴蝶。

*island 島

['aɪlənd]

They sailed from the island.
他們從這座島開船出去。

*it 它，那個東西

[ɪt]

It is your candy. 那是你的糖果。

I ate it already. 我已經吃下它了。

Phonics world

找出適當的字母填入空格中，並且連連看！

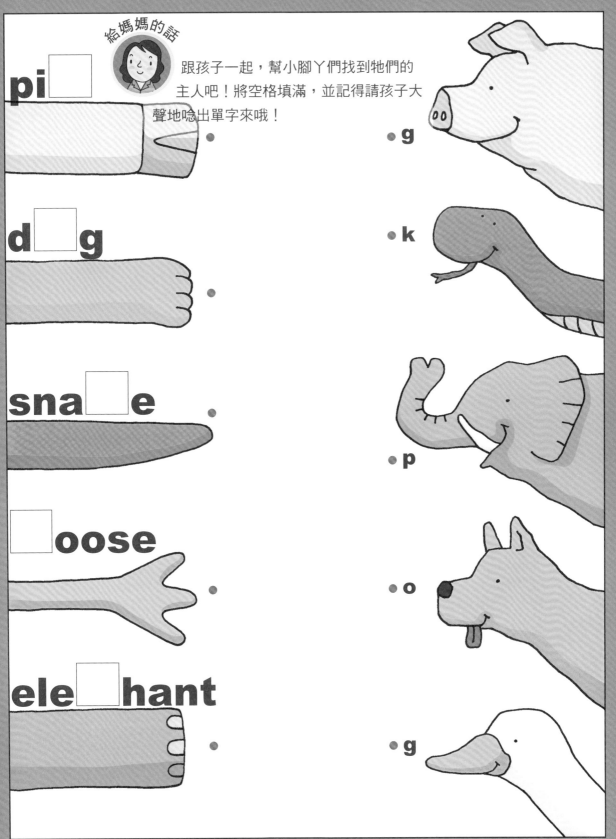

pi□

給媽媽的話

跟孩子一起，幫小腳丫們找到牠們的主人吧！將空格填滿，並記得請孩子大聲地唸出單字來哦！

• g

d□g

• k

sna□e

• p

□oose

• o

ele□hant

• g

給媽媽的話

首先，找一張舒適的沙發或椅子，靠在床頭也可以。
放鬆心情，讓孩子依偎在懷裡。帶著孩子一起唸生字，
生字旁如果有插圖，唸完生字後，
請用生動活潑的語調講解插圖，增進孩子連結圖像與聲音的記憶能力。

J j [ʤe]

jacket 夾克
[ˈʤækɪt]

I need a new jacket.
我需要一件新夾克。

jam 果醬
[ʤæm]

Would you pass me the strawberry jam?
你可以把草莓果醬遞給我嗎？

January 一月
[ˈʤænjuˌɛrɪ]

The baby was born in January.
那個寶寶在一月出生。

jeans 牛仔褲

[ʤɪnz]

How about this pair of jeans?
這件牛仔褲怎麼樣？

blue jeans 藍色牛仔褲

*job 工作

[ʤɑb]

I am looking for a job. 我正在找工作。

*join 參加

[ʤɔɪn]

Join with us today! 今天就加入我們吧！

joke 玩笑

[ʤok]

This is a joke. 這是一個玩笑。

joy 歡樂，高興

[ʤɔɪ]

He was filled with joy. 他充滿歡喜。

*juice 果汁

[ʤus]

Have a fruit or juice at the breakfast daily.
每天早餐吃顆水果或喝杯果汁。

July 七月
[ʤuˈlaɪ]

I will go to Paris in July. 我七月將會去巴黎。

*jump 跳躍
[ʤʌmp]

How high can you jump?
你可以跳多高？

June 六月
[ʤun]

The gallery will open in June. 美術館將在六月開幕。

*jungle 叢林
[ˈʤʌŋgl̩]

A crocodile lives in the jungle.
鱷魚住在叢林裡。

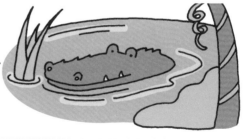

*just 剛才；只
[ʤʌst]

I have just arrived at home. 我剛到家。

JOB
職業

人小志氣高，問問孩子將來長大後想做什麼（**What do you want to do when you grow up?**），讓孩子用英文回答 **I want to be a _____ when I grow up.**。找找看圖片裡有沒有孩子想要從事的職業，這個職業都做哪些工作呢？

sailor
船員

photographer
攝影師

farmer
農夫

musician 音樂家

dancer
舞蹈家

firefighter
消防員

actor
演員

bus driver
公車司機

teacher
老師

computer programmer
電腦程式設計師

pilot 飛行員

carpenter 木匠

singer 歌手

nurse 護士

doctor 醫師

HOSPITAL

BAKERY

chef 主廚

baker 麵包師傅

policeman 警察

OPEN

RESTAURANT

首先，找一張舒適的沙發或椅子，靠在床頭也可以。
放鬆心情，讓孩子依偎在懷裡。帶著孩子一起唸生字，
生字旁如果有插圖，唸完生字後，
請用生動活潑的語調講解插圖，增進孩子連結圖像與聲音的記憶能力。

K k [ke]

kangaroo 袋鼠

[ˋkæŋgəˋru]

Kangaroos are cute.
袋鼠很可愛。

★keep 保持

[kip]

Keep silence while a baby is sleeping.
當小嬰兒睡覺時請保持安靜。

Keep a promise. 信守諾言。

kettle 水壺

[ˋkɛt!]

The kettle begins to boil.
水壺的水要燒開了。

*key 鑰匙

[ki]

Without the key, nobody can get in.
沒有鑰匙，就沒有人能進去。

*kick 踢

[kɪk]

Don't kick at a dog.
不要踢狗。

*kid 小孩

[kɪd]

We have no kids.
我們沒有小孩。

*kill 殺

[kɪl]

I don't want to kill time.
我不想殺時間（浪費時間）。

*kind 親切的，和藹的

[kaɪnd]

You are very kind. 你很親切。

⭑king 國王 ⊙ queen

[kɪŋ]

The king was very greedy.
這個國王非常貪心。

kiss 親吻

[kɪs]

May I kiss you? 我可以吻你嗎？

⭑kitchen 廚房

[ˈkɪtʃɪn]

Who is there in the kitchen? 誰在廚房裡？

⭑knee 膝蓋

[ni]

My dog likes to sleep on my knees.
我的狗喜歡在我的膝蓋上睡覺。

⭑knife 刀子

[naɪf]

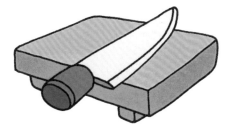

I need a sharp knife.
我需要一把尖刀。

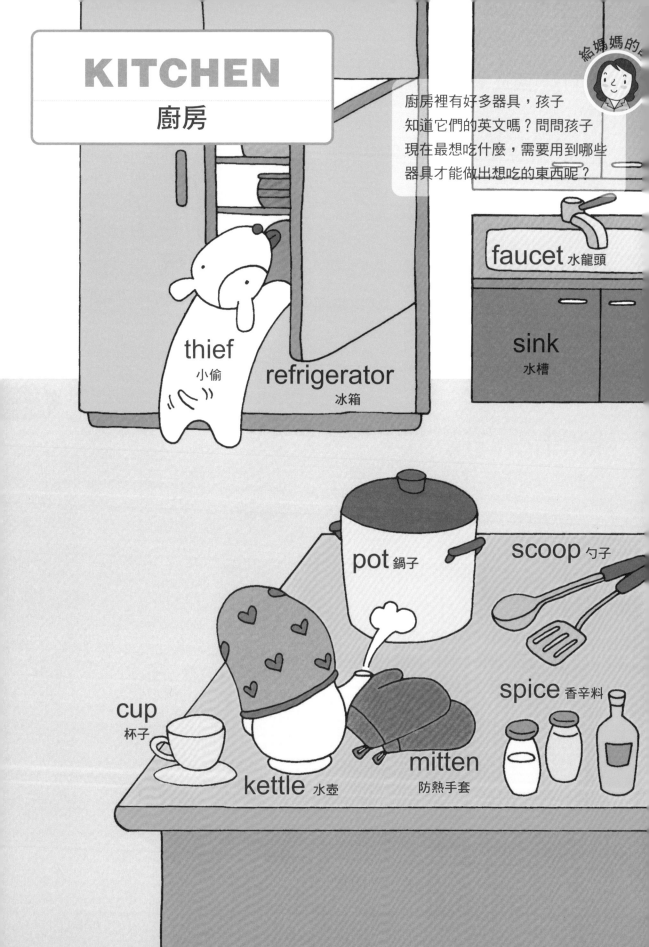

KITCHEN
廚房

給媽媽的

廚房裡有好多器具,孩子
知道它們的英文嗎?問問孩子
現在最想吃什麼,需要用到哪些
器具才能做出想吃的東西呢?

faucet 水龍頭

sink 水槽

thief 小偷

refrigerator 冰箱

pot 鍋子

scoop 勺子

spice 香辛料

cup 杯子

kettle 水壺

mitten 防熱手套

＊knock 敲

[nɑk]

Knock the door before you come in.
進門前請先敲門。

＊know 知道；認識

[no]

Do you know my name? 你知道我的名字嗎？

Know yourself. 認識你自己。

Korea 韓國

[kəˊrɪə]

I live in Korea.
我住在韓國。

 前面的單字「knee，knife，knock，know」中，有些奇怪的地方，你發現了嗎？單字明明是 k 開頭，念起來卻沒有「k」的發音。像這樣的情形，我們稱 k 叫做「無聲子音」，也就是指「沒有聲音的發音」的意思。

带著孩子一起做練習，從迷宮的入口處開始。經過圖片時，看看孩子唸不唸得出對應圖片的生字，並將空格填滿。如果孩子唸不出，再唸給孩子聽。一定要填對字母，才能繼續往下走喔。

給媽媽的話

Phonics world
空格中填入適當的字母

k□ng

ke□

□nk

□orea

□am

king, ink, key, Korea, jam

[ɛl]

✱lady 小姐 ⬌ gentleman

[ˈledɪ]

Suzzie is a sweet young lady.
蘇西是位可愛的年輕小姐。

✱lake 湖

[lek]

Let's swim in the lake.
我們在湖裡游泳吧。

✱lamp 燈

[læmp]

Put a lamp beside the window.
放一盞燈在窗邊。

185

*land 土地
[lænd]

He has his own land.
他有自己的土地。

language 語言
['læŋgwɪʤ]

How many different languages can you speak?
你能說多少不同的語言？

*large 大的
[lɑrʤ]

Your garden is very large. 你的花園非常大。

*last 最後的
[læst]

It is your last chance! 這是你最後的機會！

*late 慢的，遲的
[let]

Why are you so late?
你為什麼這麼慢？

I was late for school this morning.
我今天早上上學遲到了。

∗laugh 笑 ● cry

[læf]

He laughs loudly. 他笑得很大聲。

∗lead 帶領，領導

[lid]

Lead your brother to the school.
帶你弟弟去學校。

∗leaf 葉子

[lif]

Suzzie found a four-leaf clover. 蘇西找到了一株幸運草。

∗learn 學習

[lɝn]

What did you learn today?
你今天學了什麼？

I am learning to dance.
我正在學跳舞。

∗leave 離開

[liv]

Teddy left New York for London.
泰迪離開紐約去倫敦。

*left 左邊；左邊的

[lɛft]

Turn left. 向左轉。

*leg 腿

[lɛg]

A deer has four legs. 一隻鹿有四條腿。

*lesson 課

[ˈlɛsn̩]

My mother teaches lessons in music.
我媽媽教音樂課。

*let 讓

[lɛt]

Let me go home! 讓我回家！

Let him stay here. 讓他留在這裡。

*letter 信

[ˈlɛtɚ]

I will never write a letter to you.
我絕不會寫信給你。

*library 圖書館

[ˈlaɪˌbrɛrɪ]

There is no library near here. 這裡附近沒有圖書館。

*lie 謊言

[laɪ]

Don't tell a lie. 別說謊。

life 生命

[laɪf]

You saved my life. 你救了我的命。

*light 燈光

[laɪt]

Turn on the light. 把燈打開。

We can't see anything without light.
沒有燈光我們無法看見任何東西。

*like 喜歡

[laɪk]

I like you. 我喜歡你。

I like ice cream. 我喜歡冰淇淋。

lily 百合花

[ˈlɪlɪ]

There are many lilies in the garden.
花園裡有很多百合花。

*line 隊伍；電話

[laɪn]

Don't cut in the line. 不要插隊。

Please hold the line. 請不要掛斷電話。

*lion 獅子

[ˈlaɪən]

Yesterday, I saw a lion in the zoo.
昨天，我在動物園看到一隻獅子。

*lip 嘴唇

[lɪp]

Don't bite your lips. 別咬你的嘴唇。

*list 清單

[lɪst]

Mom makes a list whenever she goes to the market.
媽媽每次去市場都會列一張清單。

*listen 聽

[ˈlɪsṇ]

I am listening to the music.
我正在聽音樂。

Listen to the radio.
聽廣播。

*little 小的

[ˈlɪtl]

Suzzie has a little bird. 蘇西有一隻小鳥。

★live 住；活著 ⊕ die

[lɪv]

Where do you live? 你住哪裡？

location 地點

[loˊkeʃən]

a good location for school 對學校來說是個好地點

above : a rainbow above the roof 屋頂上的一道彩虹

on : a boat on the river 河上的一艘船

in : a key in the bag 袋子裡的一把鑰匙

beside : a baby beside me 我旁邊的一個寶寶

under : a rabbit under the tree 樹下的一隻兔子

a bird above the cloud 雲朵上的一隻鳥

a cock on the roof 屋頂上的一隻公雞

a chimney under the cloud 雲朵下的一根煙囪

a tree behind the house 屋子後面的一棵樹

a dog beside the house 屋子旁邊的一隻狗

Suzzie in the house 屋子裡的蘇西

flowers on the ground 地上的花

✴long 長的 ● short

[lɔŋ]

How long is the ladder?
這個梯子有多長？
My house is a long way from school.
我的家離學校很遠。

✴look 看

[lʊk]

Look at me. 看著我。

A baby looked me in the face. 一個寶寶看著我的臉。

✴lose 遺失

[luz]

Don't lose the money. 別把錢弄丟。

✴lot 很多

[lɑt]

There are a lot of cats in my house.

我家有很多隻貓。

✴loud 大聲的

[laʊd]

Teddy can make loud whistles.
泰迪可以吹出大聲的口哨。

*love 愛 ⊖ hate

[lʌv]

I love you, Mom. 我愛你，媽媽。

*low 低的 ⊖ high

[lo]

I heard a low laugh. 我聽到一陣低沉的笑聲。

The prices are low. 價格很低廉。

L

*luck 運氣

[lʌk]

Good luck! 祝你好運！

*lunch 午餐

[lʌntʃ]

Have you enjoyed
   your lunch at the park?
你在公園享用午餐了嗎？

首先，找一張舒適的沙發或椅子，靠在床頭也可以。
放鬆心情，讓孩子依偎在懷裡。帶著孩子一起唸生字，
生字旁如果有插圖，唸完生字後，
請用生動活潑的語調講解插圖，增進孩子連結圖像與聲音的記憶能力。

M m [ɛm]

✳ma'am 小姐；女士

[mæm]

Is Suzzie present? 蘇西在嗎？ Yes, ma'am. 是的，小姐。

女士稱呼為 ma'am，男士則稱呼 sir。

✳machine 機器

[məˈʃin]

Many things are made by machines.
很多東西是機器做的。

✳mad 發狂的

[mæd]

a mad man 一個發狂的男人

magic 魔術

[ˈmædʒɪk]

Magic is a trick. 魔術是一種技法。

195

*mail 郵件

[mel]

I get a lot of mail every day.
我每天都收到許多郵件。

Suzzie had seventeen voice mail.
蘇西有十七封語音留言。

*make 製造；做

[mek]

Let's make a kite. 我們來做風箏吧。

*man 男人 ● woman

[mæn]

This man is a genius.
這男人是個天才。

*many 許多的 ● few

[ˊmɛnɪ]

I want to travel to many places. 我想要去很多地方旅行。

*map 地圖

[mæp]

We need a map when we travel.
旅行時我們需要地圖。

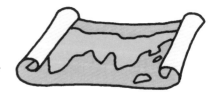

✳March 三月

[mɑrtʃ]

You can't see me from March to June.
三月到六月你沒有辦法見到我。

小寫的 march 則是指「行進」的意思，請牢記這兩種用法。

✳market 市場

[ˊmɑrkɪt]

Where is the market? 市場在哪裡？

✳marry 嫁；娶

[ˊmærɪ]

Would you marry me?
你願意嫁給我嗎？

✳matter 事情

[ˊmætɚ]

What is the matter with you?
你怎麼了（什麼事情困擾你了）？

✳May 五月

[me]

We can see roses in May.
五月時我們可以看到玫瑰。

*may 可能，也許；可以

[me]

He may come back today.
他可能今天回來。

It may be true.
那也許是真的。

May I sing a song here?
我可以在這裡唱一首歌嗎？

maybe 也許；大概

[´mebɪ]

Maybe I can help you. 也許我可以幫助你。

me 我

[mi]

Give me a cup of milk. 給我一杯牛奶。

Teddy doesn't like me. 泰迪不喜歡我。

*meat 肉

[mit]

You should eat more vegetables than meat.
你應該吃多點蔬菜甚過於吃肉。

*medal 獎牌；勳章

[´mɛdḷ]

a prize medal 一枚獎章

✱meet 認識；會見

[mit]

It is very nice to meet you.
非常高興認識你。

When can we meet?
我們何時能見面 ？

✱melon 香瓜

[ˈmɛlən]

a slice of melon 一片香瓜

menu 菜單

[ˈmɛnju]

May I have the menu, please? 可以給我菜單嗎？

merry 興高采烈的

[ˈmɛrɪ]

I wish you a Merry Christmas!
我祝你聖誕快樂！

✱meter 公尺

[ˈmitɚ]

The river is thirty meters long.
這條河長三十公尺。

*middle 中間；中間的

['mɪdl̩]

A cat sat down in the middle of the room.
一隻貓坐在房間的中央。

*milk 牛奶

[mɪlk]

I like milk.
我喜歡牛奶。

*million 一百萬

['mɪljən]

three million people 三百萬人

mine 我的

[maɪn]

This piano is mine. 這架鋼琴是我的。

*minute 分鐘

['mɪnɪt]

Would you wait for about five minutes?
你可以等大約五分鐘嗎？

＊mirror 鏡子

['mɪrɚ]

Let's hang a mirror on the wall.
我們掛一面鏡子在牆上吧。

＊Miss 小姐

[mɪs]

Miss Johnson teaches me ballet.
強森小姐教我跳芭蕾舞。

＊model 模型；模特兒

['mɑdl̩]

a model of a ship
一艘船的模型

＊mom / mommy 媽媽

[mɑm / 'mɑmɪ]

Where are you going, mom? 媽媽，你要去哪裡？

My mom is beautiful. 我的媽媽很美麗。

Monday 星期一

['mʌnde]

I will meet Suzzie next Monday.
我下星期一會和蘇西見面。

*money 金錢

[ˈmʌnɪ]

Do you have any money? 你有沒有錢？

*monkey 猴子

[ˈmʌŋkɪ]

Monkeys like bananas.
猴子喜歡香蕉。

*month 月份

[mʌnθ]

I will stay here for two months. 我會留在這裡兩個月。

*moon 月亮，月球

[mun]

Does a rabbit really live in the moon?
真的有一隻兔子住在月亮上嗎？

Someday we can go to the moon.
有一天我們能去月球。

*morning 早上，早晨

[ˈmɔrnɪŋ]

I go to a mountain every Sunday morning.
我每個星期天早晨都會去爬山。

Get up early in the morning.
早上要早起。

mosquito 蚊子

[məsˊkito]

There are lots of mosquitoes in the garden.
花園裡有很多蚊子。

Nowadays we can see mosquitoes in winter.
現在我們可以在冬天看到蚊子。

✳mother 母親，媽媽

[ˊmʌðɚ]

My mother is a singer.
我的母親是一名歌星。

✳mountain 山

[ˊmaʊntṇ]

The mountain is covered with snow. 山上蓋滿了雪。

mouse 老鼠 mice

[maʊs]

A cat is looking for a mouse.
一隻貓正在找尋老鼠。

若為複數（兩隻以上的老鼠）時，寫法為 mice [maɪs]。

✳mouth 嘴巴

[maʊθ]

Open your mouth wide. 把你的嘴巴張大。

A frog has a big mouth. 青蛙有一張大嘴巴。

*move 移動；搬動

[muv]

Don't move your hand. 不要移動你的手。

Suzzie moved her chair nearer to the fire.
蘇西把她的椅子搬近火旁邊。

We are going to move next week. 我們下星期將要搬家。

*movie 電影

[ˈmuvɪ]

I am fond of movies.
我喜歡電影。

*Mr. 先生

[ˈmɪstɚ]

Mr. Smith lives alone. 史密斯先生一個人住。

*Mrs. 太太

[ˈmɪsɪz]

Mrs. Smith 史密斯太太

Ms. 小姐，女士

[mɪz]

Ms. Smith is very kind. 史密斯小姐人非常好。

*much 許多的，大量的

[mʌtʃ]

How much money do you have?
你有多少錢？

How much is it? 它要多少錢？

much 適用在不可細數的事物，many 則適用在可以細數的事物。

mushroom 蘑菇

[ˈmʌʃrum]

A mushroom looks like an umbrella.
蘑菇看起來像雨傘。

*music 音樂

[ˈmjuzɪk]

Do you like music? 你喜歡音樂嗎？

*must 必須

[mʌst]

You must go at once. 你必須馬上去。

my 我的

[maɪ]

This is my dog. 這是我的狗。

You are my good friend.
你是我的好朋友。

N n [ɛn]

nail 指甲；釘子
[nel]

Don't chew your nails.
別咬你的指甲。

fingernail 手指甲

toenail 腳趾甲

Would you bring me some nails? 你可以帶給我一些釘子嗎？

*name 名字
[nem]

What is your name? 你叫什麼名字？

My name is Suzzie. 我的名字叫蘇西。

*narrow 狹窄的 ↔ wide, broad
[ˈnæro]

This road is narrow. 這條路很窄。

nation 國家；國民

[ˈneʃən]

the Korean nation
韓國國民

*near 附近 ● far

[nɪr]

Suzzie lives near my house. 蘇西住在我家附近。

Is there any post offices near here?
這裡附近有郵局嗎？

*neck 脖子

[nɛk]

Mom wears a scarf around her neck.
媽媽圍一條圍巾在她的脖子上。

a necklace 一條項鍊

a necktie 一條領帶

*need 需要

[nid]

I need some carrots. 我要一些紅蘿蔔。

needle 針

[ˈnidl̩]

Find a needle around you. 在你附近找一根針。

neighbor 鄰居

[ˈnebɚ]

Be kind to the neighbors. 對鄰居要親切。

a good neighbor 一個好鄰居

neither 兩者都不；也不

[ˈniðɚ]

Neither story is true.
兩個故事都不是真的

*never 從來沒有；絕不

[ˈnɛvɚ]

I have never seen a dragon.
我從來沒有看過龍。

Never hit your sister again.
不要再打你的妹妹

*new 新的 ⊝ old

[nju]

This is a new boat. 這是一艘新船。

I want to buy a new violin.
我想要買一把新的小提琴。

*news 消息；新聞

[njuz]

Bad news travels quickly.
壞消息傳得快。

Is there any news?
有任何消息嗎？

newspaper 報紙

['njuz,pepɚ]

Why do you rip my newspaper? 你為什麼撕我的報紙？

*next 下一個

['nɛkst]

Who is the next? 下一位是誰？

We are going to go on a picnic next week.
我們下星期即將要去郊外野餐。

*nice 好的

[naɪs]

Teddy is really nice.
泰迪人真好。

Your present is very nice.
你的禮物非常不錯。

*night 晚上 ⊖ day

[naɪt]

I can't sleep alone at night. 晚上我沒有辦法一個人睡。

nine 九

[naɪn]

I spent nine months in India.
我在印度待了九個月

*no 不；沒有的

[no]

I have no idea. 我不知道。

No, it isn't mine. 不，那不是我的。

*noise 噪音；喧鬧聲

[nɔɪz]

Don't make a noise at night. 晚上不要製造噪音。

noon 下午

[nun]

Teddy didn't get up until noon.
泰迪直到中午才起床。

*north 北邊

[nɔrθ]

a north wind 一陣北風

North Pole 北極

*nose 鼻子

[noz]

I don't like my big nose. 我不喜歡我的大鼻子。

*not 不，不是

[nɑt]

It is not my fault. 那不是我的錯。

I can not stay here. 我無法留在這裡。

*notebook 筆記本

[ˈnotˌbʊk]

Open your notebook. 打開你的筆記本。

nothing 沒有；沒事

[ˈnʌθɪŋ]

Ask me nothing.
不要問我任何事。

Nothing is impossible.
沒有事是不可能的。

⋆November 十一月

[noˈvɛmbɚ]

It is the third of November today.
今天是十一月三日。

⋆now 現在，馬上

[naʊ]

Do your homework, now!
馬上去做你的功課！

⋆number 數字；號碼

[ˈnʌmbɚ]

What is your cellphone number?
你的手機號碼是幾號？

⋆nurse 護士

[nɝs]

I want to be a nurse.
我想成為一位護士。

nut 堅果

[nʌt]

Where can I buy nuts?
我在哪裡可以買到堅果？

時鐘裡，日曆上，電話上，溫度計裡，數字無所不在。請孩子找出家裡哪邊有數字，並說出這些數字的英文。與孩子玩猜數字的遊戲，由家長或孩子在 **0** 到 **100** 裡選一個數字，再由另一方來猜。比如，家長選 **15**，孩子猜 **60**，家長就要說 **between zero and sixty**（在 **0** 和 **60** 之間），孩子再從這個範圍裡猜，直至猜中 **15** 為止。記得要用英文喔！

0	zero		
1	one	第一	first
2	two	第二	second
3	three	第三	third
4	four	第四	fourth
5	five	第五	fifth
6	six	第六	sixth
7	seven	第七	seventh
8	eight	第八	eighth
9	nine	第九	ninth
10	ten	第十	tenth
11	eleven	第十一	eleventh
12	twelve	第十二	twelfth
13	thirteen	第十三	thirteenth
14	fourteen	第十四	fourteenth
15	fifteen	第十五	fifteenth
16	sixteen	第十六	sixteenth
17	seventeen	第十七	seventeenth

18	eighteen	第十八	eighteenth
19	nineteen	第十九	nineteenth
20	twenty	第二十	twentieth
21	twenty-one	第二十一	twenty-first
22	twenty-two	第二十二	twenty-second
23	twenty-three	第二十三	twenty-third
24	twenty-four	第二十四	twenty-fourth
25	twenty-five	第二十五	twenty-fifth
30	thirty	第三十	thirtieth
40	forty	第四十	fortieth
50	fifty	第五十	fiftieth
60	sixty	第六十	sixtieth
70	seventy	第七十	seventieth
80	eighty	第八十	eightieth
90	ninety	第九十	ninetieth
100	one hundred	第一百	one hundredth
200	two hundred	第二百	two hundredth

Oo

object 目標

[ˈɑbdʒɪkt]

> We must have an object in life.
> 我們在生活中必須要有一個目標。

ocean 海洋

[ˈoʃən]

> Whales live in the ocean. 鯨魚住在海洋裡。

＊o'clock 點鐘

[əˈklɑk]

> It is five o'clock. 現在是五點鐘。

October 十月

[ɑkˈtobɚ]

> We have a midterm examination in October.
> 我們十月有一個期中考。

∗of …的；其中的

[ɑv]

What color of T-shirt is he wearing?
他現在穿的 T 恤顏色是什麼？

One of us should go to the store.
我們當中的一個人應該要去那家店。

∗off 從…離開

[ɔf]

Teddy fell off a ladder. 泰迪從梯子上跌落。

Get off the bus at the next station.
下一站要下車。

∗office 辦公室

[ˈɔfɪs]

Father is still in the office.
父親仍然在辦公室裡。

∗often 常常

[ˈɔfən]

Teddy often visits Suzzie. 泰迪常常拜訪蘇西。

How often do you go to the movies? 你多久看一次電影？

∗oh 噢

[o]

Oh God! 噢，我的天啊！　　Oh yes! 噢，太棒了！

∗oil 油

[ɔɪl]

This fruit contains oil. 這種水果含有油脂。

∗OK / okay 可以，很好，順利

[oˊke]

Can I call you later? 我待會可以打電話給你嗎？

It's okay with me. 可以，我沒關係。

Everything is OK. 每件事都很好。

∗old …歲；老的 ● young

[old]

O

I am ten years old. 我十歲。

Suzzie is an old friend of mine.
蘇西是我的一個老朋友。

∗on 在…之上

[ɑn]

Put your pen on the desk.
把你的筆放在桌上。

There is a swan on the lake.
湖上有一隻天鵝。

*once 曾經；一次

[wʌns]

There was once a giant. 曾經有一個巨人。

I saw a snail only once. 我只有看過蝸牛一次。

one –

[wʌn]

One and one make two.
一加一就變成二。

*only 只有

[ˈonlɪ]

I will tell it only to you. 我只對你說這件事。

*open 打開 ● close

[ˈopən]

Open your mind. 打開你的心。

Open your mouth wide. 把你的嘴巴張大。

May I open the window? 我可以把窗戶打開嗎？

*or 或是

[ɔr]

Answer yes or no. 回答是或不是。

Which do you like better,
apples or bananas?
蘋果或香蕉，你比較喜歡哪一個？

*orange 橘子;橘色;橘色的

[ˋɔrɪndʒ]

Teddy ate too many oranges.
泰迪吃太多橘子了。

organ 管風琴

[ˋɔrgən]

Suzzie is playing the organ.
蘇西正在彈管風琴。

O

ostrich 鴕鳥

[ˋɑstrɪtʃ]

The ostrich has two toes on each foot.
鴕鳥每隻腳有二個腳趾頭。

*other 其他

[ˋʌðɚ]

I have some other things to do.
我有其他的事情要做。

our 我們的

[aʊr]

Our team won. 我們的隊伍贏了。

This is our church. 這是我們的教會。

*out 在外 ○ in

[aʊt]

Let's go out for a walk. 我們到外面散步吧。

Don't go out. 別出去外面。

outside 外面，外部 ○ inside

[ˈaʊtˈsaɪd]

It is very cold outside.
外面非常冷。

There is a monster outside the house.
房子外面有一隻野獸。

oven 烤箱

[ˈʌvən]

Mother bought a new oven. 媽媽買了一台新烤箱。

*over 在⋯之上 ○ under

[ˈovɚ]

The clouds are over my head.
雲在我的頭上。

The plane is flying over the sea.
飛機正飛過大海。

owl 貓頭鷹

[aʊl]

Owls don't sleep at night.
貓頭鷹不在晚上睡覺。

own 自己的

[on]

Suzzie has her own style.
蘇西有她自己的風格。

OX 公牛

[ɑks]

Teddy is as strong as an ox.
泰迪和一頭公牛一樣強壯。

給媽媽的話

首先，找一張舒適的沙發或椅子，靠在床頭也可以。
放鬆心情，讓孩子依偎在懷裡。帶著孩子一起唸生字，
生字旁如果有插圖，唸完生字後，
請用生動活潑的語調講解插圖，增進孩子連結圖像與聲音的記憶能力。

P p [pi]

*page 頁，頁碼

[pedʒ]

Open your book, page 10.
翻開你的書，第十頁。

*paint 油漆；繪畫

[pent]

We painted the walls white.
我們把牆壁漆成白色。

*pair 一對，一雙

[pɛr]

three pairs of shoes 三雙鞋

a pair of earrings 一對耳環

pajamas 睡衣

[pə'dʒæməs]

Why are you still wearing your pajamas?
為什麼你還穿著睡衣？

★pants 褲子

[pænts]

Put on your pants. 穿上你的褲子。

★paper 紙；報紙；報告

['pepɚ]

two sheets of paper 兩張紙

Would you look through the papers?
你會看這些報告嗎？

★pardon 原諒，寬恕

['pɑrdn̩]

Pardon me. 原諒我（請再說一次）。

★parents 父母

['pɛrənts]

Parents always love us. 父母親總是愛著我們。

Let's write a letter to our parents.
我們寫一封信給我們的父母吧。

*park 公園
[pɑrk]

We walked slowly to the park. 我們慢慢走向公園。

There is no parks near my house.
我家附近沒有公園。

*party 宴會；派對
[ˈpɑrtɪ]

Will you come to my birthday party?
你會來我的生日派對嗎？

*pass 走過；傳遞
[pæs]

A big bear passed by me. 一隻大熊走過我身旁。

Pass me the salt. 把鹽巴遞給我。

*pay 支付
[pe]

How much do I pay for it?
我要支付多少錢？

*peace 和平
[pis]

Doves are a symbol of peace.
鴿子是和平的象徵。

peach 桃子

[pitʃ]

We can eat peach in summer.
夏天我們可以吃到桃子。

peacock 孔雀

[ˈpikɑk]

Where can I see a peacock?
我在哪裡能夠看到孔雀呢？

peanut 花生

[ˈpiˌnʌt]

Is there any peanut butter? 有沒有花生醬？

P

*pear 西洋梨

[pɛr]

I bought some pears. 我買了些西洋梨。

*pen 筆

[pɛn]

You have many pens.
你有很多支筆

★pencil 鉛筆

[ˈpɛnsl̩]

Pencils are made of wood.
鉛筆是木頭做的。

★people 人種；人們

[ˈpipl̩]

the peoples of Asia 亞洲的人種

There are many people in town on Saturday.
星期天有很多人在鎮上。

pepper 胡椒

[ˈpɛpɚ]

Add salt and pepper, please.
請加鹽巴和胡椒。

perhaps 也許

[pɚˈhæps]

Perhaps that is true. 也許那是真的。

person 人

[ˈpɝsn̩]

This person needs your help.
這個人需要你的幫助。

He is a famous person.
他是一位有名的人。

pet 寵物
[pɛt]

Do you like pets?
你喜歡寵物嗎？

Pets are not allowed to come into this store.
寵物不准進入這家店。

phone 電話
[fon]

What's your phone number? 你的電話號碼是幾號？

*piano 鋼琴
[pɪˈæno]

I like playing the piano.
我喜歡彈鋼琴。

*pick 挑選
[pɪk]

Don't pick the apples. 不要挑選這些蘋果。

*picnic 野餐
[ˈpɪknɪk]

We will go on a picnic tomorrow. 我們明天會去野餐。

*picture 圖畫

[ˈpɪktʃɚ]

Draw your own pictures. 畫你自己的圖。

pie 派

[paɪ]

How about some tomato pie?
來點蕃茄派如何？

*piece 片；張；塊

[pis]

a piece of paper 一張紙

a piece of cake 一塊蛋糕

*pig 豬

[pɪg]

A pig loves to eat.
豬很愛吃。

*pilot 飛行員

[ˈpaɪlət]

My brother is a pilot.
我的哥哥是一名飛行員

✳pin 插上；別上

[pɪn]

Let me pin a rose on your dress.
讓我在妳的洋裝上別一朵玫瑰花吧。

✳pine 松樹

[paɪn]

We planted some pine trees in the garden.
我們在花園裡種了些松樹。

pineapple 鳳梨

[ˊpaɪnˊæpl]

Will you make me some pineapple juice?
你可以幫我打些鳳梨汁嗎？

P

✳pink 粉紅色；粉紅色的

[pɪŋk]

I have many pink dresses.
我有很多粉紅色的衣服。

✳pipe 導管

[paɪp]

a water pipe 一根水管

pizza 披薩
['pitsə]

May I order a pizza?
我可以點一份披薩嗎？

＊place 地方；位置
[ples]

What a nice place! 好棒的地方！

＊plan 計畫
[plæn]

We are planning to visit Europe this winter.
我們正計畫今年冬天去歐洲玩。

＊plane 飛機
[plen]

Be quiet on a plane.
在飛機上要安靜。

＊plant 栽種，播種
[plænt]

Let's plant seeds in the backyard.
我們在後院播種吧。

*play 演奏；玩
[ple]

Suzzie is good at playing the violin.
蘇西擅長演奏小提琴。

You cannot play baseball in the garden.
你不能在花園裡玩棒球。

player 演奏家；球員
[ˈpleɚ]

a piano player
一位鋼琴演奏家

He is a great baseball player.
他是一位偉大的棒球球員。

*please 請，拜託；取悅
[pliz]

Please, give me a chance. 拜託，給我一個機會。

Your song pleases me. 你的歌讓我很開心。

*pocket 口袋
[ˈpɑkɪt]

What do you have in your pocket?
你的口袋裡有什麼？

✱point 重點；尖端；指點
[pɔɪnt]

What is your point? 你的重點是什麼？

Be careful, the point is sharp. 小心，這個尖頭很利。

It is rude to point your finger at a person.
將你的手指頭指著別人是很粗魯的。

✱police 警察
[pəˈlis]

Where are the police? 警察在哪裡？

polite 禮貌的
[pəˈlaɪt]

Suzzie is a polite girl. 蘇西是位有禮貌的女孩。

pond 池塘
[pɑnd]

They are digging
    a pond in the backyard.
他們正在後院挖一座池塘。

✱pool 池子
[pul]

How deep is this pool? 這個池子有多深？

＊poor 貧窮的 ● rich ；可憐的
[pur]

The beggar is poor. 那個乞丐很可憐。

pork 豬肉
[pork]

Would you like to have pork?
你要吃豬肉嗎？

Muslims do not eat pork.
回教徒不吃豬肉。

＊post 郵寄
[post]

I forgot to post this letter. 我忘了寄這封信。

＊poster 海報
['postɚ]

We can see many posters on the wall.
我們可以在牆上看到許多海報。

pot 罐子
[pɑt]

Candies are in the pot.
糖果在罐子裡。

*potato 馬鈴薯
[pə′teto]

Can you peel the potatoes? 你可以削馬鈴薯嗎？

*practice 練習
[′præktɪs]

You must practice harder. 你必須更努力練習。

*present 禮物
[′prɛznt]

I don't need any presents.
我不需要任何禮物。

*pretty 漂亮的
[′prɪtɪ]

What a pretty cat it is! 這隻貓好漂亮啊！

Suzzie is a pretty girl. 蘇西是一個漂亮的女孩。

*print 列印
[prɪnt]

Would you print this page for me?
你可否印這一頁給我？

＊problem 問題
['prɑbləm]

a social problem 一個社會問題

Do you have any problems? 你有什麼問題嗎？

What is the problem? 問題是什麼？

＊pull 拉
[pʊl]

Pull this string. 拉這條帶子。

Don't pull my hair. 不要拉我的頭髮。

pumpkin 南瓜
['pʌmpkɪn]

A pumpkin changed into a carriage.
一顆南瓜變成了一輛馬車。

P

puppy 小狗
['pʌpɪ]

My grandmother gave me a puppy for a present.
我奶奶送我一隻小狗當作禮物。

purple 紫色；紫色的
['pɝpl̩]

A violet is purple.
紫羅蘭是紫色的。

*push 推
[pʊʃ]

Push the door.
推開這扇門。

We pushed Teddy out of the room.
我們把泰迪推出了房間。

*put 放
[pʊt]

Put the vase on the table.
將花瓶放在桌上。

Don't put your hands in your pocket.
別把你的手放在口袋裡。

puzzle 猜謎
[ˈpʌzl̩]

Teddy enjoys puzzles.
泰迪喜歡猜謎。

P

首先，找一張舒適的沙發或椅子，靠在床頭也可以。
放鬆心情，讓孩子依偎在懷裡。帶著孩子一起唸生字，
生字旁如果有插圖，唸完生字後，
請用生動活潑的語調講解插圖，增進孩子連結圖像與聲音的記憶能力。

quarter 四分之一；十五分鐘，一刻鐘
[ˈkwɔrtɚ]

It is a quarter past five.
現在是五點十五分。

*queen 皇后；女王⟷ king
[kwin]

a queen of flowers
花中之后

The queen has three princesses.
那位皇后有三個公主。

*question 問題
[ˈkwɛstʃən]

May I ask a question? 我可以問一個問題嗎？

Your questions are difficult. 你的問題很難。

*quick 快速的
[kwɪk]

Teddy is quick in action.
泰迪動作很快。

quickly 快速地，立即，馬上
[ˈkwɪklɪ]

Can you finish your work more quickly?
你可以快一點完成你的工作嗎？

The bats fly quickly.
蝙蝠飛得很快。

*quiet 安靜的
[ˈkwaɪət]

Be quiet.
安靜。

This is a quiet place.
這是個安靜的地方。

Write the missing letters
空格中填入漏掉的字母

給媽媽的話

帶著孩子一起做練習，先看看孩子唸不唸得出圖片的內容，再沿著梯形迷宮
找出對應圖片的生字，並將空格填滿。如果孩子唸不出，再唸給孩子聽。

☐ueen   pu☐pkin   ☐x   pi☐za

給媽媽的話

首先，找一張舒適的沙發或椅子，靠在床頭也可以。

放鬆心情，讓孩子依偎在懷裡。帶著孩子一起唸生字，

生字旁如果有插圖，唸完生字後，

請用生動活潑的語調講解插圖，增進孩子連結圖像與聲音的記憶能力。

R r [ɑr]

rabbit 兔子

[ˈræbɪt]

Rabbits have long ears.
兔子有長長的耳朵。

race 比賽；種族

[res]

The turtle won the race. 烏龜贏了這場比賽。

the race problem 種族問題

★radio 收音機

[ˈredɪˌo]

Mom is listening to the radio.
媽媽正在聽收音機。

railroad 鐵路

['rel,rod]

Walking along the railroad is dangerous.
沿著鐵路走很危險。

*rain 下雨

[ren]

It rains. 下雨了。

A snail is always waiting for raining.
蝸牛總是在等下雨。

*rainbow 彩虹

['ren,bo]

A rainbow is above the clouds.
彩虹在雲的上面。

raise 舉起，抬起

[rez]

Raise your cup. 舉起你的杯子。

Can you raise your voice? 你可以把你的音量提高嗎？

*read 閱讀

[rid]

Suzzie is reading a book loudly.
蘇西正在大聲讀一本書。

⋆ready 準備好的
['rɛdɪ]

Are you ready for school?
你準備好去學校了嗎？

When will it be ready?
何時才會準備好呢？

⋆real 真正的，真實的
['riəl]

real gold 真金

really 真正地
['rɪəlɪ]

Really? 真的嗎？

I am really glad to meet you. 我真的很高興見到你。

That's really nice. 那樣真好。

R

receive 收到 ● give
[rɪ'siv]

I received a letter from my friend.
我從朋友那裡收到了一封信。

Did you receive my present?
你收到我的禮物了嗎？

*record 記錄

[rɪˊkɔrd]

Someone recorded your speech.
有人錄下了你的談話。

*red 紅色；紅色的

[rɛd]

a red rose 一個紅鼻子

He turned red with anger. 他氣得臉色泛紅。

refrigerator / fridge 冰箱

[rɪˊfrɪdʒə‚retə / frɪdʒ]

Put your ice cream into the
refrigerator quickly.
快把你的冰淇淋放進冰箱。

*remember 記得 ⊖ forget

[rɪˊmɛmbə]

Do you remember his phone number? 你記得他的電話號碼嗎？

I don't remember who did it. 我不記得那是誰做的。

*repeat 重覆

[rɪˊpit]

Repeat these sentences three times.
重覆這些句子三次。

✳rest 休息
[rɛst]

You need some rest.
你需要休息一下。

✳restaurant 餐廳
[ˈrɛstərənt]

Let's go to the Chinese restaurant tonight.
我們今晚去中國餐館吃飯吧。

✳return 返回；歸還
[rɪˈtɜn]

Teddy returned to New York.
泰迪回紐約了。

Do I have to return this book to the library?
我必須把這本書歸還給圖書館嗎？

R

✳ribbon 絲帶
[ˈrɪbən]

Where did you buy this ribbon?
妳在哪裡買這條絲帶？

Suzzie is wearing a yellow ribbon in her hair.
蘇西綁著一條黃絲帶在頭髮上。

*rice 稻米

[raɪs]

Asian people live on rice.
亞洲人以米為主食。

*rich 富有的，有錢的 ● poor

[rɪtʃ]

Teddy is rich. 泰迪很富有。

*ride 騎

[raɪd]

I ride on a bicycle to school.
我騎腳踏車上學。

*right 右邊；右邊的 ● left

[raɪt]

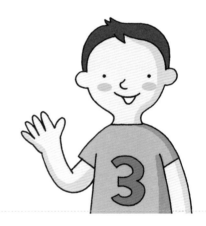

Raise your right hand.
舉起你的右手。

*ring 戒指

[rɪŋ]

a wedding ring 一枚結婚戒指

I lost my ring. 我丟了我的戒指。

*river 河

[ˈrɪvɚ]

Teddy swims in the river.
泰迪在河裡游泳。

*road 馬路，街道

[rod]

Go straight along this road. 沿著這條路直走。

*robot 機器人

[ˈrobət]

This robot can speak a few words.
這個機器人可以說一些話。

*rock 岩石

[rɑk]

A snake is on the rock. 一條蛇在岩石上。

*rocket 火箭

[ˈrɑkɪt]

The Chinese launched
a rocket to the moon.
中國人發射了一枚火箭到月球上。

*roll 滾動

[rol]

A coin rolled on the floor.
一枚硬幣滾落在地上。

*roof 屋頂

[ruf]

A dove disappeared on the roof.
一隻鴿子在屋頂上消失了。

*room 房間

[rum]

Clean up your room. 清理好你的房間。

Is Suzzie in the room? 蘇西在房間裡嗎？

R

*rose 玫瑰

[roz]

Roses are one of the most
        beautiful flowers.
玫瑰是最美的花之一。

*round 圓的

[raʊnd]

The earth is round like an orange.
地球圓圓的就像一粒橘子。

rule 規矩

[rul]

the rules of the class
班級公約

*ruler 尺

[ˈrulɚ]

Can I borrow your ruler?
我可以借你的尺嗎？

*run 跑

[rʌn]

I had to run to catch the dog.
我必須跑去抓狗。

給媽媽的話

首先，找一張舒適的沙發或椅子，靠在床頭也可以。
放鬆心情，讓孩子依偎在懷裡。帶著孩子一起唸生字，
生字旁如果有插圖，唸完生字後，
請用生動活潑的語調講解插圖，增進孩子連結圖像與聲音的記憶能力。

★sad 傷心的，悲哀的 ⊖ glad

[sæd]

Why are you sad? 你為何傷心？

sad news 悲哀的消息

★safe 安全的；無損的 ⊖ dangerous

[sef]

a safe place 一個安全的地方

Is it safe to use? 那個東西可以安全使用嗎？

★salad 沙拉

[ˈsæləd]

Let's order fruit salad, too.
我們也點水果沙拉吧。

sale 賣；銷售
[sel]

a cash sale 現金交易

The shoes are on sale today. 鞋子今天在拍賣。

＊salt 鹽
[sɔlt]

A baby spilt salt.
一個寶寶把鹽撒了出來。

Put the salt, please.
請放鹽。

＊same 同樣的
[sem]

Teddy and I are of the same age. 泰迪和我同樣年紀。

We eat the same food every day.
我們每天吃同樣的食物。

＊sand 沙子；沙灘
[sænd]

He is lying on the sands. 他正躺在沙灘上。

sandwich 三明治
[´sændwɪtʃ]

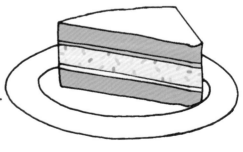

I had sandwiches for lunch.
我午餐吃三明治。

Saturday 星期六

[ˈsætɚde]

What are you going to do on Saturday night?
你星期六晚上打算做什麼？

sausage 香腸

[ˈsɔsɪdʒ]

Pork is used to make sausages.
豬肉可用來製作香腸。

*say 說

[se]

What did you say? 你說了什麼？

Teddy said that I was pretty. 泰迪說我很漂亮。

*school 學校

[skul]

Where is your school?
你的學校在哪裡？

School opens tomorrow.
學校明天開學。

science 科學

[ˈsaɪəns]

My favorite subject is science.
我最喜歡的科目是科學。

scissors 剪刀

['sɪzɚz]

Cut out the paper with scissors.
用剪力把紙剪開。

*score 分數

[skor]

Teddy won by a score of 1 to 0.
泰迪以一比零的分數獲勝。

*sea 海

[si]

These animals live in the deep sea.
這些動物住在深海裡。

*season 季節

['sizn̩]

the rainy season 雨季

Autumn is the best
    season to take a trip.
秋天是旅行的最佳季節。

Which season do you like best?
你最喜歡哪一個季節？

∗seat 座位
[sit]

Have a seat, please. 請坐。

Where is your seat? 你的座位在哪裡？

∗see 看見
[si]

Can you see something? 你能看見什麼東西嗎？

I saw you go out yesterday.
我昨天看見你外出。

∗sell 賣
[sɛl]

Do you sell sugar? 你有賣糖嗎？

∗send 寄
[sɛnd]

Send us an e-mail.
寄一封電子郵件給我們。

He sent roses to me.
他寄玫瑰花給我。

September 九月
[sɛpˈtɛmbɚ]

We moved into a new house in September.
我們在九月時搬進了一間新房子。

SEASON
季節

spring 春天

January 一月
February 二月
March 三月

summer 夏天

April 四月
May 五月
June 六月

一年有四季，一季有三月。哪些月屬於哪個季節呢？春天適合從事
什麼活動，秋天適合從事什麼活動呢？問問孩子最想在哪個季節做
哪些事，並帶領孩子認識十二個月份的英文。

July 七月
August 八月
September 九月

autumn / fall 秋天

October 十月
November 十一月
December 十二月

winter 冬天

✱service 服務；招待

['sɝvɪs]

The service is good at this hotel. 這家旅館的服務很好。

✱set 一部；一副；安置

[sɛt]

a chess set 一盤棋局

Would you set a glass on the table?
你可以在桌上放一個玻璃杯嗎？

settle 沉澱；安放

['sɛtl̩]

The rain will settle the dust.
這場雨會使灰塵沉澱下來。

seven 七

['sɛvn̩]

There are seven gates. 有七道門。

sew 縫合，縫上

[so]

You have to sew
a button on the coat.
你得在外套上縫上一個鈕扣。

＊shall 應該；必須

[ʃæl]

You shall succeed this time. 你這次必須成功。

shampoo 洗髮精

[ʃæmˊpu]

This shampoo smells good.
這罐洗髮精聞起來不錯。

＊shape 形狀

[ʃep]

The shape of Italy is like a boot. 義大利的形狀像一個靴子。

What shape is it? 那是什麼形狀？

＊she 她

[ʃi]

She is smart. 她很聰明。

She is kind. 她人很親切。

＊sheep 綿羊

[ʃip]

A farmer has fifty sheep.
一個農夫有五十隻綿羊。

✴sheet 一張；床單

[ʃit]

　　two sheets of paper 二張紙

✴ship 船

[ʃɪp]

　　It is the biggest ship in the world.
　　那是世界上最大的船。

　　the ship's journal 航行日誌

✴shirt 襯衫

[ʃɝt]

　　Your shirt is dirty. 你的襯衫很髒。

✴shoe 鞋子

[ʃu]

　　a pair of shoes 一雙鞋

　　Take off your shoes, please.
　　請脫鞋。

✴shoot 發射，射出

[ʃut]

　　Suzzie shot an arrow into the air.
　　蘇西向空中射出一支箭。

*shop 商店

[ʃɑp]

a gift shop 一家禮品店

Let's go shopping tomorrow.
我們明天去逛街吧。

*short 短的 ⊕ long；矮的 ⊕ tall

[ʃɔrt]

short hair 短髮

Today was a short day.
今天過得很快。

My father is a short man.
我的父親是矮個子。

should 應該

[ʃud]

You should work now. 你現在應該工作了。

What should we do? 我們應該做什麼呢？

*shoulder 肩膀

[ˈʃoldɚ]

A bird is sitting on his shoulder. 一隻鳥正站在他的肩膀上。

*shout 喊叫，大聲叫

[ʃaʊt]

He shouted that I was a liar.
他大叫說我是個騙子。

*show 出示；給…看

[ʃo]

Teddy showed me a book. 泰迪給我看一本書。

Show me the ticket, please. 請出示門票。

*shower 淋浴，洗澡

[ˈʃaʊɚ]

Small drops make a shower.
積少成多。

*shut 關上 ⬌ open

[ʃʌt]

Shut the door, please. 請把門關上。

*sick 生病的

[sɪk]

Teddy is sick. 泰迪生病了。

My brother is often sick. 我的弟弟常常生病。

*side 旁邊；邊；面
[saɪd]

We have to paint both sides of the fence.
我們必須油漆籬笆的兩邊。

I thought you were on my side. 我以為你站在我這一邊。

Which side do I play? 我在哪一邊比賽？

*sign 記號，符號；簽名
[saɪn]

a traffic sign 一個交通號誌

Would you sign your name on the check?
你可以在支票上簽名嗎？

silence 沉默
['saɪləns]

Suzzie is sitting there in silence.
蘇西正沉默地坐在那裡。

*silver 銀；銀色；銀幣 ● gold
['sɪlvɚ]

The stars are twinkling like silver.
星星像銀幣一樣閃耀著。

*sing 唱歌

[sɪŋ]

What shall we sing? 我們應該唱什麼呢？

Let's sing the happy birthday
    song for Suzzie.
我們為蘇西唱生日快樂歌吧。

*sir 先生；長官

[sɝ]

I got lost, sir. 我迷路了，先生。

男士稱為 sir，女士則稱為 ma'am。

*single 單一的；個別的

['sɪŋgl̩]

a single room 一間單人房

*sister 姐姐；妹妹

['sɪstɚ]

My sister can't sleep without her cat.
我妹妹沒有她的貓就睡不著。

*sit 坐

[sɪt]

Sit down, please. 請坐下。

Sit up straight. 要坐端正。

six 六

[sɪks]

You didn't call me for six days.
你六天沒有打電話給我了。

★size 尺寸，大小

[saɪz]

What is the size of the earth? 地球有多大呢？

What size do you wear in shoes? 你穿幾號的鞋子？

★skate 溜冰鞋；溜冰

[sket]

Put on your skates quickly.
快穿上你的溜冰鞋。

I love to skate.
我喜歡溜冰。

ski 滑雪

[ski]

Let's go skiing.
我們去滑雪吧。

skin 表皮；皮膚

[skɪn]

a banana skin 一片香蕉皮；一個尷尬或麻煩的處境

What would be good for my skin? 什麼東西對我的皮膚好？

✴skirt 裙子

[skɝt]

Suzzie doesn't like putting on a skirt.
蘇西不喜歡穿裙子。

✴sky 天空

[skaɪ]

Why is the sky blue? 為什麼天空是藍色的？

✴sleep 睡覺

[slip]

Did you sleep well last night?
你昨晚睡得好嗎？

I'm sleepy. 我好睏。

✴slide 滑動

[slaɪd]

The snow slid off the roof. 雪從屋頂滑落。

✴slow 慢的 ● fast

[slo]

Why did you run so slow?
為什麼你跑得這麼慢？

slowly 慢慢地

['slolɪ]

They walked slowly to the park.
他們慢慢地走到公園。

*small 小的，小型的 ⊕ big, large

[smɔl]

What a small world it is! 世界真小呀！

I made a small cage for the bird.
我為那隻鳥做了一個小籠子。

Your hands are too small.
你的手太小了。

*smell 聞起來；察覺出

[smɛl]

These white roses smell sweet.
這些白玫瑰聞起來很香甜。

*smile 微笑

[smaɪl]

Suzzie smiled to see me.
蘇西微笑著看我。

*smoke 冒煙；抽菸

[smok]

This stove smokes badly. 這個火爐冒煙冒得很厲害。

Does your father smoke? 你的爸爸抽菸嗎？

snail 蝸牛

[snel]

Have you ever eaten snails?
你曾經吃過蝸牛嗎？

snake 蛇

[snek]

Snakes have no feet. 蛇沒有腳。

*snow 雪；下雪

[sno]

It is snowing. 下雪了。

*so 非常，如此；所以

[so]

I am so sorry. 我非常抱歉。

I don't think so. 我不這麼認為。

It's raining, so I will stay at home all day.
下雨了，所以我會整天待在家裡。

*soap 肥皂

[sop]

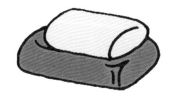

Wash your hands well with soap.
用肥皂把你的手洗乾淨。

＊soccer 足球

[ˈsɑkɚ]

Soccer is popular in the world.
足球在全世界很風行。

＊sock 襪子

[sɑk]

Where is my socks?
我的襪子在哪裡？

＊sofa 沙發

[ˈsofə]

A cat is sleeping on the sofa. 一隻貓正在沙發上睡覺。

soft 柔軟的 ● hard

[sɔft]

A baby has soft skin. 寶寶有柔軟的皮膚。

Mom's voice was soft. 媽媽的聲音很輕柔。

soldier 士兵

[ˈsoldʒɚ]

He must be a soldier.
他一定是一位士兵。

*some 一些，部分

[sʌm]

Mom gave me some money today.
媽媽今天給了我一些錢。

something 某些事物

[ˈsʌmθɪŋ]

Is there something to eat?
有什麼東西可以吃嗎？

I am sure that I lost something.
我確定我丟了什麼東西。

sometimes 有時候

[ˈsʌmˌtaɪmz]

Teddy comes to visit me sometimes.
泰迪有時候會來看我。

somewhere 在某處

[ˈsʌmˌhwɛr]

I found the ring somewhere around here.
我在這附近找到了這枚戒指。

*son 兒子 ⊙ daughter

[sʌn]

Like father, like son.
有其父必有其子。

∗song 歌曲

[sɔŋ]

We have never heard your song.
我們從來沒有聽過你的歌。

Which song do you like best?
你最喜歡哪一首歌？

∗soon 很快地

[sun]

Suzzie will come soon. 蘇西很快就會來。

∗sorry 對不起；感到抱歉的

['sɑrɪ]

Sorry! 對不起！

I am sorry. 我很抱歉。

I am sorry for you. 我對你感到抱歉。

∗sound 聲音；聽起來

[saund]

I can hear the sound of flowing water.
我可以聽到流水的聲音。

∗soup 湯

[sup]

What do you put in the soup? 你在湯裡放什麼東西？

swimming 游泳

ski 滑雪

golf 高爾夫

football / soccer 足球

baseball 棒球

running 跑步

SPORT
運動

bowling 保齡球

tennis 網球

boxing 拳擊

wrestling 摔角

basketball

籃球

ballet 芭蕾

ping-pong 乒乓球

volleyball 排球

sour 酸的，酸味的

[saʊr]

a sour apple 一顆青蘋果

These grapes are sour.
這些葡萄很酸。

＊south 南方；南方的 ● north

[saʊθ]

South Australia is a good place to live.
南澳洲是個適合居住的好地方。

＊space 空白；篇幅；太空

[spes]

You can write on both sides of the paper
if you need more space.
如果你需要更多位置來寫的話，你可以寫在這張紙的正反兩面。

Someday we can travel into space.
有朝一日，我們可以到外太空旅遊。

spaghetti 義大利麵

[spə´gɛtɪ]

We had spaghetti for dinner.
我們晚餐吃了義大利麵。

sparrow 麻雀

['spæro]

Sparrows are chirping.
麻雀吱吱喳喳地說話。

*speak 說話

[spik]

This baby cannot speak yet. 這個寶寶還不會說話。

Do you want to speak a foreign language?
你想要說某種外語嗎？

special 特別的

['spɛʃəl]

a special talent 一項特殊才能

Are you looking for something special?
你正在找一些特別的東西嗎？

speech 演講

[spitʃ]

He made an opening speech.
他發表了一場公開演說。

*speed 速度

[spid]

Safety is more important than speed. 安全比速度還重要。

*spell 拼音

[spɛl]

How do you spell your name? 你的名字要怎麼拼？

*spend 花費；度過

[spɛnd]

Don't spend too much time on it. 別花太多時間在那上面。

How did you spend the vacation? 你怎麼度過這個假期？

spider 蜘蛛

[ˈspaɪdɚ]

A spider can spin a web.
蜘蛛能夠結網。

*spoon 湯匙

[spun]

Where are the spoons? 湯匙在哪裡？

*sport 運動；競技活動

[sport]

My favorite sport is basketball.
我最喜歡的運動是籃球。

*spring 春天

[sprɪŋ]

I want to visit here again in spring.
春天時我想再次拜訪這裡。

*square 正方形

[skwɛr]

Cut the card into a square. 把這張卡片剪成一個正方形。

*stair 樓梯；梯級

[stɛr]

A baby is crying upstairs. 一個寶寶正在樓上哭。

*stamp 郵票

[stæmp]

I am collecting stamps.
我正在蒐集郵票。

*stand 站立

[stænd]

Stand up, please. 請站起來。

This cat is too weak to stand.
這隻貓太虛弱以致於站不起來。

✳star 星星

[star]

We can see many stars in the country.
在鄉下我們可以看到很多星星。

✳start 開始

[start]

My brother started to cry. 我的弟弟開始哭了。

When do we start? 我們何時開始？

✳station 車站

[ˈsteʃən]

Where can I find the bus station? 我在哪裡可以找到公車車站？

a police station 一間警察局

✳stay 停留；暫住；待

[ste]

My uncle is staying at the hotel.
我叔叔現在暫住在旅館裡。

I stayed at home all day. 我一整天都待在家。

✳steam 蒸汽；蒸

[stim]

a rice steamer
一個蒸飯鍋

*step 步伐；步驟
[stɛp]

It is only a step to the store. 到那家店只有一步路而已。

What is the next step? 下一步是什麼呢？

*stick 枝條；拐杖
[stɪk]

Gather sticks to make a fire.
蒐集樹枝來起火。

My grandfather is walking with a stick.
我的爺爺正拿著拐杖走路。

still 仍然；靜止
[stɪl]

Teddy is still angry. 泰迪仍然在生氣。

The night is very still. 夜晚非常沉靜。

*stone 石頭
[ston]

This house is made of stone.
這間房子是石造的。

*stop 停止
[stɑp]

Mother stopped talking. 媽媽停止說話了。

∗store 商店

[stor]

There are many expensive things at that store.
那家店有很多昂貴的東西。

∗storm 暴風雨

[stɔrm]

After a storm comes a calm.
暴風雨後有寧靜。

∗story 故事

[ˊstorɪ]

I will tell you a ghost story.
我來告訴你一個鬼故事。

∗stove 爐子

[stov]

Put potatoes on the stove.
把馬鈴薯放在爐子上。

∗straight 直的；直接的

[stret]

a straight line 一條直線

a straight talk 一段坦率的談話

★strange 奇怪的

[strendʒ]

I heard a strange sound last night.
昨天晚上我聽見一個奇怪的聲音。

Your voice is strange today.
你今天的聲音很奇怪。

★strawberry 草莓

[ˋstrɔbɛrɪ]

These strawberries are fresh.
這些草莓很新鮮。

stream 溪流

[strim]

Lots of kids are swimming in the stream.
很多孩子在小溪中游泳。

★street 街道

[strit]

I met a teacher in the street. 我在街上遇到了一位老師。

★strike 擊打

[straɪk]

Don't strike the table with fist.
不要用拳頭打桌子。

Tom strikes me on the head.
湯姆打我的頭。

*strong 強壯的 ● weak

[strɔŋ]

I am strong. 我很強壯。

The strong winds were blowing last night.
昨天晚上吹著強風。

*student 學生

['stjudn̩t]

I am a student. 我是一個學生。

*study 學習

['stʌdɪ]

You must study hard. 你必須認真學習。

How do you study for this test?
這次考試你如何準備？

*stupid 愚蠢的

['stjupɪd]

How stupid you are! 你好愚蠢！

*subway 地下鐵

['sʌbˌwe]

I have to take the subway
to the church.
我必須搭地鐵去教會。

*sugar 糖

['ʃʊgɚ]

How many sugars do you take in your coffee?
你的咖啡裡放了多少糖？

*summer 夏天

['sʌmɚ]

Have a wonderful summer!
祝你有個愉快的夏天！

*sun 太陽

[sʌn]

The sun rises every day.
太陽每天昇起。

Sunday 星期日

['sʌnde]

This store is closed every Sunday.
這家店每個星期日不營業。

sunny 陽光充足的，暖和的

['sʌnɪ]

It is a sunny day. 今天是個大晴天。

＊supermarket 超級市場

[´supɚˏmɑrkɪt]

I can't find my favorite ice cream at your supermarket.
我無法在你的超市裡找到我最愛的冰淇淋。

＊supper 晚餐

[´sʌpɚ]

What's there for supper? 晚餐有什麼？

＊sure 確定的，一定的

[ʃur]

Are you sure about the phone number?
這支電話號碼你確定嗎？

He is sure to come. 他一定會來。

＊surprise 驚訝

[sɚ´praɪz]

We were surprised
    to find the house empty.
我們很驚訝地發現這棟房子是空的。

＊sweater 毛衣

[´swɛtɚ]

This sweater is not warm.
這件毛衣並不暖和。

✱sweet 甜美的；芳香的

[swit]

It smells sweet. 它聞起來很香。

Your voice is sweet. 你的聲音很甜美。

✱swim 游泳

[swɪm]

I was swimming in the lake.
我在湖裡游泳。

I can swim across the river.
我可以游過這條河。

✱swing 搖擺，擺動

[swɪŋ]

The door is swinging in the wind. 門在風中擺動著。

✱switch 開關

[swɪtʃ]

Turn on the switch. 打開開關。

首先，找一張舒適的沙發或椅子，靠在床頭也可以。
放鬆心情，讓孩子依偎在懷裡。帶著孩子一起唸生字，
生字旁如果有插圖，唸完生字後，
請用生動活潑的語調講解插圖，增進孩子連結圖像與聲音的記憶能力。

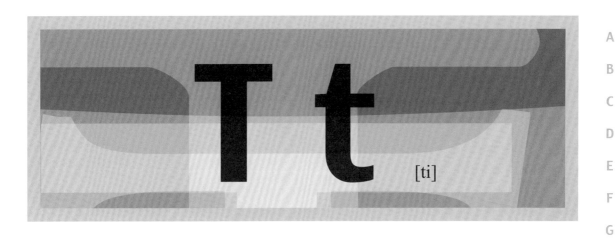

[ti]

*table 桌子

[´tebl̩]

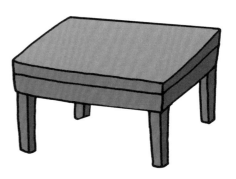

What is on the table?
桌子上有什麼？

Can you put this on the table?
你能把這個放在桌上嗎？

*take 取用；拿著

[tek]

I can't take money from you. 我不能拿你的錢。

Take it with you. 把它帶在身上。

*talk 談話

[tɔk]

He talks too much. 他話太多了。

Don't talk like that. 別那樣說話。

*tall 高大的 ⟷ short
[tɔl]

How tall are you? 你有多高？

---

*tape 錄影帶；錄音帶
[tep]

Do you want to watch *Cinderella*? I have it on tape.
你想看《灰姑娘》嗎？我有它的錄影帶。

target 靶心；目標
[ˈtɑrgɪt]

Shoot at the target. 射中靶心。

I missed the target. 我沒有射中目標。

*taste 嚐起來，品嚐
[test]

I taste garlic in it. 我有吃到大蒜。

*taxi 計程車
[ˈtæksɪ]

You can go there by taxi.
你可以搭計程車去那裡。

---

*tea 茶
[ti]

Would you have some tea with us?
你要不要跟我們一起喝個茶？

*teach 教導

[titʃ]

Mom teaches me how to swim.
媽媽教我如何游泳。

*team 隊，組

[tim]

Your team has lost. 你們那隊已經輸了。

tear 眼淚

[tɪr]

I was almost in tears. 我幾乎要哭了。

*telephone / phone 電話

[ˈtɛləˌfon / fon]

I telephoned Teddy to come here at once.
我打電話給泰迪叫他馬上來這裡。

Pick up the phone. 接電話。

*television / TV 電視

[ˈtɛləˌvɪʤən / ˈtiˈvi]

Turn off the television. 關掉電視。

I didn't watch TV. 我沒有看電視。

A
B
C
D
E
F
G
H
I
J
K
L
M
N
O
P
Q
R
S
T
U
V
W
X
Y
Z

*tell 告訴

[tɛl]

Tell me your name, please.
請告訴我你的名字。

Don't tell me where I am.
別告訴我現在在那裡。

temperature 溫度，氣溫

[ˈtɛmprətʃɚ]

What is the temperature in Sahara?
撒哈拉沙漠的溫度是幾度？

*temple 殿堂；寺廟

[ˈtɛmpl̩]

a temple of art 一間充滿藝術的寺廟

ten +

[tɛn]

Let's count to ten. 我們從一數到十吧。

tender 嫩的，柔軟的

[ˈtɛndɚ]

tender meat 嫩肉

a tender skin 柔軟的皮膚

＊tennis 網球

[ˈtɛnɪs]

We played tennis yesterday.
我們昨天玩網球。

＊test 測驗

[tɛst]

a blood test 驗血

study for the test 為考試而讀書

＊than 比…還，比較

[ðæn]

I am older than you.
我比你老。

Teddy is taller than me.
泰迪比我還高。

＊thank 感謝

[θæŋk]

Thank you for your letter. 謝謝你寫信給我。

＊that 那個，那個東西

[ðæt]

Can you see that? 你可以看到那個東西嗎？

What is that? 那是什麼？

＊the 這；那

[ðə / ði]

I keep a dog. The dog is white.
我有一隻狗。這隻狗是白色的。

theater 戲院；劇院

[ˊθɪətɚ]

Where is the theater? 戲院在哪裡？

What was the name of the theater? 那間劇院的名字是什麼？

＊then 還有；那麼

[ðɛn]

She was beautiful, then. 還有，她很美麗。

Don't cry, then I will give you some chocolate.
你不哭，我就給你一些巧克力。

＊there 那裡 ● here

[ðɛr]

I will be there in a minute.
我一分鐘後會到那裡。

＊they 他們

[ðe]

They were thieves. 他們是小偷。

*thick 厚的；粗的 ● thin

[θɪk]

a thick book 一本厚書

a thick line 一條粗線

---

thief 小偷 thieves

[θif]

A thief usually visits at night.
小偷通常夜間來光顧。

「竊盜集團」或是二個以上的小偷，則是用 thieves（thief 的複數型態）表示。

---

*thin 瘦的；細的 ● thick

[θɪn]

Your fingers are really thin. 你的手指真是纖細。

*thing 東西

[θɪŋ]

What's that thing in your hand?
你手裡拿著的那個東西是什麼？

apple

tree

There is a name for every thing.
每件事物都有一個名字。

⋆think 想

[θɪŋk]

I think it is true. 我想那是真的。

I didn't think to find you here. 我沒想到在這裡能找到你。

⋆thirsty 口渴的

['θɝstɪ]

I am thirsty. 我口渴了。

⋆this 這個 ⬌ that

[ðɪs]

This is my book. 這是我的書。

This is my sister. 這是我的姐姐。

these [ðiz]（this 的複數型態）表示「這些」的意思。

⋆thousand 一千

['θaʊzn̩d]

Thousands of cattle died.
數以千計的牛隻死了。

⋆throw 丟

[θro]

Don't throw a stone to a cat. 不要對貓丟石頭。

Throw a bone to a dog. 丟根骨頭給狗。

thumb 姆指

[θʌm]

My thumb is too big.
我的姆指太大了。

★ticket 門票；車票

[ˈtɪkɪt]

a concert ticket 一張音樂會門票

How do you get the tickets? 你如何拿到車票的？

★tie 綁住，拴起

[taɪ]

Let's tie a dog to a tree. 我們把一隻狗拴在樹上吧。

Teddy tied his brother's hands together.
泰迪把他弟弟的手綁在一起。

★tiger 老虎

[ˈtaɪgɚ]

Have you ever seen
    a tiger close at hand?
你有近距離看過老虎嗎？

★till 直到

[tɪl]

I can't wait till next year. 我不能等到明年。

My sister did not come till ten o'clock.
我姐姐直到十點才來。

*time 時間

[taɪm]

What time is it now?
現在是幾點？

*tired 累的，疲倦的

[taɪrd]

Suzzie was tired from homework.
蘇西做功課做得累了。

*to 到

[tu]

The tree fell to the ground. 這顆樹倒在地上了。

Turn to the right. 向右轉。

*today 今天

[tə´de]

Today is my birthday. 今天是我的生日。

Why did you tell a lie today? 你今天為什麼要說謊？

toe 腳趾

[to]

the little toe 小腳趾

No birds have more than four toes.
沒有鳥有超過四個腳趾。

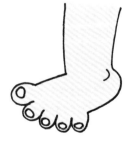

★together 一起

[tə'gɛðɚ]

Let's stay here together.
我們一起留在這裡吧。

toilet 馬桶；廁所

['tɔɪlɪt]

Always flush the toilet. 每次都要沖馬桶。

★tomato 番茄

[tə'meto]

I always drink
tomato juice every morning.
我每天早上都喝番茄汁。

★tomorrow 明天 ⊙ yesterday

[tə'mɔro]

What do I have to do tomorrow? 我明天必須做什麼？

I won't go to school tomorrow. 我明天不會去學校。

tongue 舌頭

[tʌŋ]

The color of your tongue is strange.
你舌頭的顏色很奇怪。

*tonight 今晚

[tə´naɪt]

It will rain tonight. 今晚會下雨。

*too 太；也

[tu]

I was late for school, too. 我上學也遲到了。

You eat too much. 你吃太多了。

*tooth 牙齒 teeth

[tuθ]

You have a sweet tooth. 你很愛吃甜食。

It is time to brush your teeth. 該是你刷牙的時間了。

牙齒的複數是 teeth [tiθ]

a front tooth 一顆門牙，a canine tooth 一顆犬齒

a bad tooth 一顆壞牙，a milk tooth 一顆乳牙，a molar tooth 一顆臼齒

a permanent tooth 一顆恒齒，a wisdom tooth 一顆智齒

a false tooth 一顆假牙

*top 頂端，上面

[tɑp]

What can you see at the top of the tree?
你在樹上可以看到什麼？

Suzzie is at the top of her class.
蘇西是她班上的第一名。

∗touch 觸摸

[tʌtʃ]

Don't touch it. 不要觸摸那個東西。

Someone touched me on the shoulder.
有人摸我的肩膀。

∗towel 毛巾

[ˈtauəl]

Would you give me a clean towel? 你可以給我一條乾淨的毛巾嗎？

∗town 小鎮

[taun]

Father has his office in town.
爸爸在小鎮裡有辦公室。

∗toy 玩具

[tɔɪ]

This train is just a toy.
這輛火車只是一個玩具。

∗train 火車

[tren]

We traveled by train in Europe.
我們在歐洲搭火車旅行。

I got up early, so I didn't miss the train.
我很早起床，所以沒有錯過火車。

tr 一起發音，是類似「彳ㄨ」的中文音。

*travel 旅行

[´træv!]

Teddy is traveling in Africa. 泰迪正在非洲旅行。

*tree 樹

[tri]

a pine tree 一顆松樹

A lot of birds are sitting in the tree.
好多鳥兒站在樹上。

*trip 旅行，旅遊

[trɪp]

Let's take a trip to the future!
我們到未來世界去旅行吧！

It was certainly a good trip this time.
這次的旅行真好玩。

trouble 問題，麻煩

[´trʌb!]

I have no trouble at all. 我沒有任何問題。

What's the trouble with you? 你怎麼了？

*truck 卡車

[trʌk]

A truck will move our things for us.
卡車會為我們搬東西。

*true 真實的，確實的

[tru]

This is not true. 這不是真的。

trust 信任，倚靠

[trʌst]

Trust me. 相信我。

Don't trust chance. 不要憑靠運氣。

*try 嘗試

[traɪ]

Try it again. 再試一次。

Try doing your best. 試著盡你最大努力。

Tuesday 星期二

[ˈtjuzde]

I have a violin lesson on Tuesday.
我星期二有一堂小提琴課。

*tulip 鬱金香

[ˈtjuləp]

He gave me a bunch of tulips.
他送我一束鬱金香。

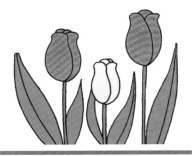

A
B
C
D
E
F
G
H
I
J
K
L
M
N
O
P
Q
R
S
T
U
V
W
X
Y
Z

turkey 火雞

['tɝkɪ]

Can a turkey fly? 火雞能飛嗎？

*turn 轉動；開啟開關

[tɝn]

Why are you turning to the left?
為什麼你要轉向左邊？

Turn the lights on.
把燈打開。

turtle 烏龜

['tɝtl̩]

**Turtles are good
　　　at swimming in the sea.**
烏龜擅長在海裡游泳。

twelve 十二

[twɛlv]

There are twelve months in a year.
一年有十二個月。

*twice 兩次

[twaɪs]

I phoned him twice.
我打了兩次電話給他。

twin 雙胞胎的

[twɪn]

My twin brother went to church instead of me.

我的雙胞胎弟弟去了教會，而不是我。

「雙胞胎」的寫法是 twins。

twinkle 閃耀

[ˈtwɪŋkḷ]

City lights twinkle at night.

城市的燈光在夜裡閃耀著。

The stars are twinkling.

星星正在閃閃發光。

two 二

[tu]

I have two dogs.

我有兩隻狗。

There are two reasons.

有兩個理由。

307

U u [ju]

ugly 醜的，難看的
[ˈʌglɪ]

This dog has an ugly face. 這隻狗有張很醜的臉。

*umbrella 雨傘
[ʌmˈbrɛlə]

I didn't bring my umbrella.
我沒有帶傘。

Take your umbrella just in case.
把你的雨傘帶著，以防萬一。

*uncle 叔叔
[ˈʌŋkl̩]

Who is your uncle?
誰是你的叔叔？

The man reading a newspaper is my uncle.
那位看報紙的男人是我的叔叔。

*under 向下；在…下面 ⊙ over

[ˊʌndɚ]

The cat is under the car. 那隻貓在車子下面。

*understand 了解，明白

[ʌndɚˊstænd]

Do you understand me? 你了解我的意思嗎？

I don't understand why you are angry at me.
我不明白你為什麼要對我生氣。

uniform 制服

[ˊjunəˌfɔrm]

Our school uniform is really pretty.
我們學校的制服真漂亮。

*until 直到

[ənˊtɪl]

Wait until two o'clock. 等到兩點鐘。

We must wait until our teacher comes.
我們必須一直等到老師來。

*up 向上；在…上方

[ʌp]

I went up to top of the mountain.
我走到山頂上。

USA 美國

[ˈjuˈɛsˈe]

Teddy lives in the USA.
泰迪住在美國。

*use 使用

[juz]

The root is used for food. 根部被拿來當作食物。

Use my pen. 用我的筆。

useful 有用的

[ˈjusfəl]

Your advice was very useful to me.
你的建議對我非常有用。

*usual 平常的

[ˈjuʒʊəl]

It is usual for me to sit up late at night.
晚上熬夜對我來說稀鬆平常。

As usual, mother forgot to lock the door.
一如往常,媽媽忘了鎖門。

usually 通常

[ˈjuʒʊəlɪ]

Usually, this street is crowded.
這條街通常擠滿了人。

I usually go to bed at ten. 我通常十點上床睡覺。

首先，找一張舒適的沙發或椅子，靠在床頭也可以。
放鬆心情，讓孩子依偎在懷裡。帶著孩子一起唸生字，
生字旁如果有插圖，唸完生字後，
請用生動活潑的語調講解插圖，增進孩子連結圖像與聲音的記憶能力。

Vv [vi]

*vacation 假期

[veˊkeʃən]

How was your summer vacation?
你的暑假過得如何？

vase 花瓶

[ves]

There is only one flower in the vase.
花瓶裡只有一朵花。

*vegetable 蔬菜

[ˊvɛdʒətəb!]

My father lives on vegetables.
我爸爸吃素。

VEGETABLE
蔬菜

garlic
大蒜

red pepper
紅色辣椒

pumpkin
南瓜

lettuce
萵苣

mushroom
蘑菇

onion
洋蔥

cucumber
黃瓜

spinach
菠菜

corn
玉米

eggplant
茄子

allium 青蔥

cabbage 甘藍菜

broccoli 花椰葉

carrot 紅蘿蔔

white radish 白蘿蔔

green pepper 青椒

pea 碗豆

tomato 番茄

potato 馬鈴薯

sweet potato 地瓜

*very 非常

[ˈvɛrɪ]

He walked very carefully.
他走路非常小心。

This question is very easy for me.
這個問題對我來說非常容易。

victory 勝利

[ˈvɪktərɪ]

Suzzie led our team to victory.
蘇西帶領我們這隊獲得勝利。

*video 錄影帶

[ˈvɪdɪˌo]

Let's stay home and watch a video. 我們留在家裡看錄影帶吧。

*view 景色，視野

[vju]

a room with a nice view 一間視野很棒的房間

*village 村莊

[ˈvɪlɪʤ]

a fishing village 一處漁村

This is the village where I was born.
這是我出生的村莊。

∗violin 小提琴

[ˌvaɪəˈlɪn]

It is difficult for Teddy to play the violin.
拉小提琴對泰迪來說並不容易。

∗visit 拜訪

[ˈvɪzɪt]

I have visited here before. 我以前拜訪過這裡。

How about visiting our new neighbors?
拜訪一下我們的新鄰居如何？

voice 聲音

[vɔɪs]

You have a good voice.
你擁有一副好嗓音。

volcano 火山

[vɑlˈkeno]

an active volcano 一座活火山

There are many active volcanoes in Hawaii.
夏威夷有很多活火山。

volleyball 排球

[ˈvɑlɪˌbɔl]

My favorite sport is volleyball.
我最喜歡的運動是排球。

首先，找一張舒適的沙發或椅子，靠在床頭也可以。
放鬆心情，讓孩子依偎在懷裡。帶著孩子一起唸生字，
生字旁如果有插圖，唸完生字後，
請用生動活潑的語調講解插圖，增進孩子連結圖像與聲音的記憶能力。

W w [ˈdʌblju]

waist 腰

[west]

Suzzie has a slender waist.
蘇西有纖細的腰。

My grandmother has no waist.
我的奶奶沒有腰身。

*wait 等待

[wet]

Don't wait if I am late. 如果我遲到了，就不要等我。

Are you waiting for someone? 你正在等人嗎？

*wake 醒來；喚醒

[wek]

Wake up! 起床！

Suzzie woke up at seven. 蘇西七點起床。

Would you wake me up at five? 你可以五點叫我起床嗎？

*walk 走路
[wɔk]

Are you going to walk or ride?
你打算走路還是騎車？

I am just walking about.
我只是去走一走。

*wall 牆
[wɔl]

Who hung this picture on the wall?
誰掛這幅畫在牆上？

*want 想要
[wɑnt]

I want to go to France. 我想要去法國。

Teddy wants me to go with him.
泰迪想要我和他一起去。

*war 戰爭
[wɔr]

The war was over. 戰爭結束了。

*warm 溫暖的
[wɔrm]

It is warm. 天氣很溫暖。

Your hands feel warm. 你的手感覺起來很溫暖。

*wash 洗

[wɑʃ]

Wash your face and hands.
去洗你的臉和手。

Please wash these clothes clean.
請把這些衣服洗乾淨。

*waste 浪費

[west]

Don't waste food. 不要浪費食物。

*watch 看；手錶

[wɑtʃ]

I watched the sun setting.
我看著太陽落下。

Teddy watches
    television every evening.
泰迪每天晚上看電視。

Where is my watch? 我的手錶在哪裡？

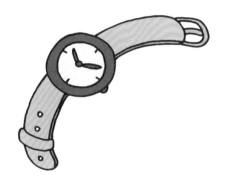

*water 水

[ˈwɔtɚ]

Fish live in the water.
魚住在水裡。

We all jumped into the water.
我們全都跳進了水裡。

watermelon 西瓜

[ˈwɔtɚˌmɛlən]

Don't cut the watermelon yet. 還不要切這顆西瓜。

wave 揮動；揮手示意

[wev]

The branches waved in the breeze.
樹枝在微風中搖曳。

Mom waved to me to go.
媽媽向我揮手表示要走了。

*way 通路；方法

[we]

I don't know the way to the station.
我不知道去車站的路。

Just do what I said; that is the best way.
就照我說的去做，那是最好的方法了。

*we 我們

[wi]

We are good friends.
我們是好朋友。

*weak 虛弱的 ↔ strong

[wik]

This dog is too weak to live long.
這隻狗太虛弱以致於不能活得久。

*wear 穿著；佩戴

[wɛr]

My sister always wears blue earrings.
我的姐姐總是戴著藍色耳環。

Father doesn't like
      wearing a ring on his finger.
爸爸不喜歡在手指上佩戴戒指。

*weather 天氣

[ˈwɛðɚ]

What is the weather like? 天氣如何？

Wednesday 星期三

[ˈwɛnzde]

See you on Wednesday. 星期三見。

*week 星期

[wik]

It is raining all this week.
整個星期都在下雨。

- Sunday 星期日　　· Monday 星期一　　· Tuesday 星期二
- Wednesday 星期三　· Thursday 星期四　· Friday 星期五
- Saturday 星期六

W

weight 重量

[wet]

What is your weight?
你有多重？

My sister wants to lose weight.
我的姐姐想要減肥。

*welcome 歡迎

[ˈwɛlkəm]

Welcome home! 歡迎回家！

Welcome to Taiwan! 歡迎來到台灣！

*well 很好地；充分地

[wɛl]

Teddy speaks French well. 泰迪法語說得很好。

My brother sleeps well. 我哥哥睡得很好。

*west 西邊

[wɛst]

The sun sets in the west.
太陽在西邊沉落。

wet 濕的；潮濕的

[wɛt]

My socks are still wet.
我的襪子還是濕的。

My brother wet his bed last night.
我弟弟昨天晚上尿床了。

whale 鯨魚

[hwel]

What do whales eat?
鯨魚吃什麼呢？

★what 什麼；多少；多麼，何等

[hwɑt]

What is this? 這是什麼？

What is your name? 你叫什麼名字？

What are you talking about? 你在說什麼？

What is the price? 價錢是多少？

What do you think of this book? 你覺得這本書怎麼樣？

What a beautiful flower it is! 這朵花好漂亮啊！

★when 何時

[hwɛn]

When did you come back? 你何時回來？

I don't know when to go. 我不知道何時要去。

*where 何處，在哪裡

[hwɛr]

Where do you live?
你住在哪裡？

Where do you come from?
你從哪裡來？

Where do I have to go?
我應該要去哪裡？

*which 哪一個

[hwɪtʃ]

Which do you like better, this or that?
你比較喜歡哪一個，這個或是那個？

Which apartment do you live in? 你住在哪一間公寓？

This is the book which I have chosen.
這是我挑過的書。

*white 白色；白色的

[hwaɪt]

Let's paint the walls white. 我們把牆漆成白色吧。

*who 誰

[hu]

Who is singing? 誰在唱歌？

Who knows him? 誰認識他？

Nobody knows who he was.
沒有人知道他曾經是什麼人。

W

*why 為什麼
[hwaɪ]

Why does fire burn?
為什麼火會燒起來？

Why are you here?
為什麼你在這裡？

I don't know why he can't sleep.
我不知道他為什麼睡不著。

*wide 寬廣的 ○ narrow
[waɪd]

This river is wide. 這條河很寬。

Why are you staring at me with such wide eyes?
你為什麼睜這樣大的眼睛看著我？

wife 妻子 ○ husband
[waɪf]

He loves his wife.
他愛他的妻子。

wild 野生的；狂野的
[waɪld]

W

wild animals 野生動物

wild weather 狂暴的天氣

*will 將要，將會，即將；能夠

[wɪl]

It will be fine tomorrow. 明天就好了。

I will be twelve years old next birthday.
下個生日我就十二歲了。

Will you visit my house?
你會來拜訪我家嗎？

Will you pass me the sugar?
你可以把糖遞給我嗎？

*win 贏得 ● lose

[wɪn]

You win.
你贏了。

Teddy wins a gold medal.
泰迪贏得了一面金牌。

*wind 風

[wɪnd]

There isn't much wind this morning.
今天早上沒有什麼風。

The wind is blowing.
風正在吹著。

*window 窗戶

[ˈwɪndo]

Who broke the window?
誰打破了窗戶？

*wing 翅膀

[wɪŋ]

An angel has wings. 天使有翅膀。

*winter 冬天

[ˈwɪntɚ]

How do animals spend the winter?
動物們如何過冬？

wish 祝福；希望

[wɪʃ]

I wish you a Happy New Year. 我祝你新年快樂。

What do you wish? 你想要許什麼願？

*with 與…一起 ↔ without

[wɪð]

W

I live with my grandmother.
我跟我的奶奶住在一起。

Will you come to the theater with us?
你會和我們一起去看電影嗎？

without 沒有 ⟷ with

[wɪˈðaut]

We can't live without food.
我們沒有食物就無法生存。

Without your advice, I couldn't succeed.
少了你的建議，我就不能成功。

wolf 狼

[wʊlf]

A wolf hurt my dog.
一隻狼咬傷了我的狗。

*woman 女人 ⟷ man

[ˈwʊmən]

A woman was singing in the street.
一個女人正在街上唱歌。

*wonder 納悶；想知道

[ˈwʌndɚ]

I wonder what he wants. 我很納悶他要什麼。

wonderful 很棒的，愉快的

[ˈwʌndɚfəl]

I had a wonderful time. 我享受了很愉快的時光。

What a wonderful challenge! 好棒的挑戰啊！

*wood 木頭；森林

[wʊd]

This house is made of wood.
這間房子是木造的。

The pond is in the middle
of the woods.
這座池塘位於森林的中央。

*word 字；話語

[wɝd]

an English word 一個英文字

Words without actions are of little use.
光說不練是沒有用的。

*work 工作；計算

[wɝk]

I have a lot of work to do this evening.
今天晚上我有很多工作要做。

Suzzie is working at mathematics.
蘇西正在算數學。

*world 世界

[wɝld]

You are the greatest friend in the world.
你是世界上最偉大的朋友。

331

worry 擔心

[ˈwɝɪ]

Mother will worry if we are late.
如果我們遲到了，媽媽會擔心。

Don't worry about it. 別為那件事擔心。

wrap 包裝；使全神貫注

[ræp]

Wrap it up in paper.
用紙將它包起來。

He is wrapped up in mysteries.
他沉迷於懸疑小說之中。

*write 寫

[raɪt]

I can write a letter in English.
我可以用英文寫一封信。

You may write in French.
你可以寫法文。

*wrong 錯誤的

[rɔŋ]

It is wrong to tell a lie. 說謊是錯的。

Your answer is wrong. 你的答案是錯的。

Write the missing letters

空格中填入漏掉的字母

給媽媽的話

帶著孩子一起做練習，先看
看孩子唸不唸得出對應圖片的
生字，並將空格填滿。如果孩子
唸不出，再唸給孩子聽。

v□se

vio□in

watc□

□olf

s□ider

vase, violin, watch, wolf, spider

X x [ɛks]

Xmas 聖誕節（Christmas 的縮寫）
['krɪsməs]

[ˈɛksməs]

Merry Xmas.
聖誕快樂。

X-ray X 光

[ˈɛksˈre]

We can see the inside of
a body through X ray.
我們藉由 X 光可以觀察身體的內部。

xylophone 木琴

[ˈzaɪləˌfon]

Suzzie is playing the xylophone.
蘇西正在彈木琴。

首先，找一張舒適的沙發或椅子，靠在床頭也可以。
放鬆心情，讓孩子依偎在懷裡。帶著孩子一起唸生字，
生字旁如果有插圖，唸完生字後，
請用生動活潑的語調講解插圖，增進孩子連結圖像與聲音的記憶能力。

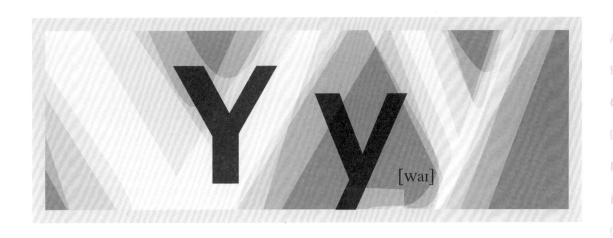

yard 庭院

[jɑrd]

The dog is barking in the yard. 這隻狗正在庭院裡叫著。

＊yeah 是（口語）⊜ yes

[jɛə]

Would you like a cup of hot chocolate?
你要來杯熱可可嗎？

Oh, yeah! 嗯，好啊！

yawn 打呵欠

[jɔn]

Teddy yawned good night.
泰迪打著呵欠說晚安。

＊year 年

[jɪr]

My brother was born two years ago.
我弟弟在兩年前出生。

✱**yellow** 黃色；黃色的

['jɛlo]

The bird in the cage is yellow.
鳥籠裡那隻鳥是黃色的。

✱**yes** 是的 ● no

[jɛs]

Is it raining? 正在下雨嗎？

Yes, it is. 是的，在下雨。

✱**yesterday** 昨天

['jɛstɚde]

Yesterday was Saturday. 昨天是星期六。

✱**yet** 還未；已經

[jɛt]

The work is not yet finished. 這個工作還沒有完成。

Have you done your homework yet? 你做你的作業了嗎？

✱**you** 你

[ju]

You are pretty. 你很漂亮。

✱**young** 年輕的 ● old

[jʌŋ]

We are young. 我們很年輕。

請跟著正確的拼字往前走

I see, follow me!

aeg

caek

brid

age

bird

cake

calor

color

evary

date

faec

every

data

daet

face

victory

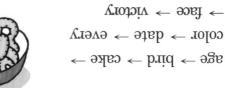

age → bird → cake →
color → date → every
→ face → victory

Zz

給媽媽的話

首先，找一張舒適的沙發或椅子，靠在床頭也可以。
放鬆心情，讓孩子依偎在懷裡。帶著孩子一起唸生字，
生字旁如果有插圖，唸完生字後，
請用生動活潑的語調講解插圖，增進孩子連結圖像與聲音的記憶能力。

Zz [zi]

zebra 斑馬
[ˈzibrə]

I saw zebras
    in the zoo yesterday.
我昨天在動物園看到斑馬。

*zero 零
[ˈzɪro]

2 minus 2 is zero. 二減二等於零。

*zoo 動物園
[zu]

There are many animals in the zoo.
動物園裡有很多動物。

ZOO
動物園

雪白的北極熊，胖嘟嘟的企鵝，貪睡的無尾熊以及虎視眈眈的鱷魚，動物園裡的動物有哪些，孩子說得出牠們的英文嗎？模仿這些動物的動作，讓孩子猜猜是哪種動物。

elephant
大象

sheep
綿羊

polar bear
北極熊

penguin
企鵝

koala
無尾熊

duck
鴨子

peacock
孔雀

alligator/crocodile
鱷魚

snake
蛇

camel
駱駝

附錄

人稱代名詞

所謂的代名詞，是指代替人或事物的用詞。

人稱代名詞所有格的變化

＜單數＞

人稱／所有格	主格（～是）	所有格（～的）	受格	所有代名詞（屬於～的）
第一人稱	I	my	me	mine
第二人稱	you	your	you	yours
第三人稱	he	his	him	his
	she	her	her	hers
	it	its	it	-

＜複數＞

人稱／所有格	主格（～是）	所有格（～的）	受格	所有代名詞（屬於～的）
第一人稱	we	our	us	ours
第二人稱	you	your	you	yours
第三人稱	they	their	them	theirs

反身代名詞

反身代名詞（人稱本身；人稱自己）

單數		複數	
I	myself	we	ourselves
you	yourself	you	yourselves
he	himself		
she	herself	they	themselves
it	itself		

不規則動詞變化

現在式	過去式	過去分詞
am	was	been
are	were	been
awake	awoke	awoken
beat	beat	beaten
become	became	become
beg	begged	begged
begin	began	begun
bend	bent	bent
bite	bit	bitten, bit
bleed	beld	beld
blow	blew	blown
break	broke	broken
bring	brought	brought
build	built	built
burn	burned, burnt	burned, burnt
buy	bought	bought
can	could	-
catch	caught	caught
choose	chose	chosen
come	came	come
cost	cost	cost
cut	cut	cut
die	dead	dead
dig	dug	dug
dive	dived, dove	dived
do / does	did	done
draw	drew	drawn
dream	dreamed, dreamt	dreamed, dreamt
drink	drank	drunk
drive	drove	driven
drop	dropped, dropt	dropped, dropt
eat	ate	eaten

附錄

現在式	過去式	過去分詞
fall	fell	fallen
feed	fed	fed
feel	felt	felt
fight	fought	fought
find	found	found
fly	flew	flown
forget	forgot	forgotten, forgot
forgive	forgave	forgiven
freeze	froze	frozen
fry	fried	fried
get	got	got, gotten
give	gave	given
go	went	gone
grow	grew	grown
hang	hung, hanged	hung, hanged
have / has	had	had
hear	heard	heard
hide	hid	hidden, hid
hit	hit	hit
hold	held	held
hop	hopped	hopped
hug	hugged	hugged
hurry	hurried	hurried
hurt	hurt	hurt
is	was	been
keep	kept	kept
know	knew	known
lay	laid	laid
lead	led	led
learn	learned, learnt	learned, learnt
leave	left	left
lend	lent	lent

現在式	過去式	過去分詞
let	let	let
lie	lay	lain
lose	lost	lost
make	made	made
may	might	-
mean	meant	meant
meet	met	met
mistake	mistook	mistaken
nod	nodded	nodded
pay	paid	paid
pin	pinned	pinned
plan	planned	planned
put	put	put
quit	quitted, quit	quitted, quit
read [i]	read [ε]	read [ε]
ride	rode	ridden
ring	rang	rung
rise	rose	risen
run	ran	run
say	said	said
see	saw	seen
sell	sold	sold
send	sent	sent
set	set	set
sew	sewed	sewed, sewn
shake	shook	shaken
shall	should	-
shine	shone	shone
shoot	shot	shot
show	showed	shown, showed
shut	shut	shut
sing	sang	sung

現在式	過去式	過去分詞
sink	sank, sunk	sunk
sit	sat	sat
skip	skipped	skipped
sleep	slept	slept
slide	slid	slid
slip	slipped	slipped
speak	spoke	spoken
spend	spent	spent
spill	spilled, spilt	spilled, spilt
spread	spread	spread
stand	stood	stood
steal	stole	stolen
stick	stuck	stuck
sting	stung	stung
stop	stopped	stopped
strike	struck	struck
swim	swam	swum
swing	swung	swung
take	took	taken
teach	taught	taught
tear	tore	torn
tell	told	told
think	thought	thought
throw	threw	thrown
understand	understood	understood
wake	waked, woke	waked, woken
wear	wore	worn
will	would	-
win	won	won
wind	wound	wound
wrap	wrapped	wrapped
write	wrote	written

CHILDREN'S DICTIONARY

國家圖書館出版品
預行編目資料

我的第一本親子英文字典 / 申仁樹著. -- 初版.--
臺北縣中和市：國際學村, 2010. 03
面；　　公分

ISBN 978-986-6829-64-2（精裝）

1. 英語 2. 字典

805.132　　　　　　　　　　　　99002784

COLUMN 單字圖庫

20個主題字庫圖像式學習，讓單字記憶更快速。

PHRASE 片語

每個單元都有一個與主題相關的片語，用圖片＋文字說明。

Idiom 片語格言輕鬆說

g face 慈眉善臉

ILLUSTRATION 圖像記憶

全彩的可愛插圖，讓唸英文就像看漫畫一樣輕鬆有趣。

VOCABULARY 字彙

列出本單元的相關字彙，照字母A-Z排列，方便記憶查詢。

用聽的也能輕鬆學
親歷其境的對話mp3
故事＋對話　學習更有趣
慢速＋正常速　練習更確實

 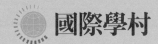

我的第一本親子英文字典
CHILDREN'S DICTIONARY

作者 WRITER	申仁樹
出版者 PUBLISHING COMPANY	台灣廣廈出版集團 TAIWAN MANSION BOOKS GROUP 國際學村出版
發行人 / 社長 PUBLISHER / DIRECTOR	江媛珍 JASMINE CHIANG
地址 ADDRESS	235新北市中和區中山路二段359巷7號2樓 2F, NO. 7, LANE 359, SEC. 2, CHUNG-SHAN RD., CHUNG-HO DIST., NEW TAIPEI CITY, TAIWAN, R.O.C.
電話 TELEPHONE NO.	886-2-2225-5777
傳真 FAX NO.	886-2-2225-8052
電子信箱 E-MAIL ADDRESS	TaiwanMansion@booknews.com.tw
網址 WEBSITE	http://www.booknews.com.tw
總編輯 CHIEF EDITOR	伍峻宏 CHUN WU
副總編輯 VICE CHIEF EDITOR	周宜珊 JOELLE CHOU
本書美術編輯 ART EDITOR	許芳莉 POLLY HSU
法律顧問	第一國際法律事務所　余淑杏律師
製版 / 印刷 / 裝訂	東豪 / 廣鑫 / 慶成
代理印務及圖書總經銷	知遠文化事業有限公司
地址	222新北市深坑區北深路三段155巷25號5樓
訂書電話	886-2-2664-8800
訂書傳真	886-2-2664-0490
出版日期	2013年2月 修訂三版九刷
郵撥帳號	18788328
郵撥戶名	台灣廣廈有聲圖書有限公司

（購書300元以內需外加30元郵資，滿300元（含）以上免郵資）